# PAPER BULLETS

## AN ABBY MAXON MYSTERY NOVEL

### ANNIE REED

TVp
Thunder Valley
Press

# PRAISE FOR ANNIE REED

"I personally think that Annie Reed is one of the best writers of her generation."

— KRISTINE KATHRYN RUSCH, AWARD-
WINNING WRITER/EDITOR

"You can't go wrong with Annie Reed. Her deftly-crafted tales—with characters as memorable as the stories themselves—far surpass most of what's out there. She deserves a wide audience."

— MICHAEL J. TOTTEN, AUTHOR

"Annie's writing is magic, seriously."

— ROBERT J. MCCARTER, AUTHOR

"Annie Reed is considered by many to be one of the best new writers appearing in fiction."

— DEAN WESLEY SMITH, EDITOR
*PULPHOUSE FICTION MAGAZINE*

# ALSO BY ANNIE REED

*A Death in Cumberland*

*Faster*

*Road of No Return*

*A Christmas Reunion*

UNEXPECTED SERIES

*Unexpected Aliens*

*Unexpected Monsters*

*Unexpected Holidays*

*Unexpected Criminals*

*Unexpected Good Guys*

*Unexpected Futures*

*Unexpected Encounters*

*Unexpected Hauntings*

*Unexpected Travels*

*Unexpected Families*

*Unexpected Critters*

*Unexpected Killers*

*Unexpected Christmas*

*Unexpected Cats*

*Unexpected Santas*

COLLECTIONS

*Crimes of Yesteryear*

*Everyday Magic*

*Life with Cats*

*Magic of the Heart*

*Turning the Page*

*Eight from the Silver State*

*The Patient Z Files*

*The Forever Soldier and Other Future Tales*

## WRITING AS KRIS SPARKS

*Shadow Life*

## WRITING AS LIZ McKNIGHT

*Wedding Belle Blues*

# PAPER BULLETS

# 1

The last thing I wanted to do on a hot Saturday afternoon in August was meet with my ex-husband. I'd spent the morning shopping with my clothes-conscious teenage daughter, Samantha, just the two of us along with about a million other parents and kids crowding the aisles in Target for a little last-minute back-to-school shopping. We also had a messy house we needed to wrestle into shape before tomorrow when her boyfriend and his mother would be in town for a visit. And to top it all off, I had a date in a few hours, and I needed time to transform myself from a sweaty, frizzy-haired mom into actual date material.

But then Ryan had called and said the only thing guaranteed to interrupt my day: "I need your help."

So here I sat in a nice air-conditioned Starbucks, ready to meet my ex and offer whatever assistance he needed.

Yes, there are days I feel like Abby Maxon, World's Biggest Sap. Why do you ask?

At least we weren't meeting in the Starbucks where I sometimes had coffee with Kyle.

Kyle Beecham's my boyfriend, and boy does it feel weird to

acknowledge that I actually have a boyfriend. Kyle's a detective with the Sparks Police Department, and we've been dating semi-seriously since the first of the year. He's a busy cop and single dad. I'm a busy private detective and single mom. It's a wonder we have time for anything other than a quick coffee at Starbucks. Tonight was one of our rare Saturday night dates, and I wasn't about to blow him off, no matter what Ryan needed.

I'd arrived a few minutes before we were scheduled to meet, so I grabbed a table near the back. Starbucks wasn't crowded, wonder of wonders, but the line at the drive-through was a good ten cars deep. I wasn't surprised. August in Nevada is not for the faint of heart. When I'd pulled in the parking lot, my car had helpfully told me it was ninety-five degrees. Drive-throughs do a bang up business during the dog days of summer when people don't want to leave the comfort of their air-conditioned cars.

I thought about ordering myself an iced latte—the aroma of fresh-ground coffee was making my mouth water—but I hoped I wouldn't be here that long. Ryan was punctual to a fault, and he'd always been a man who got right to the point.

Except, apparently, for today.

I'd just looked at my watch for the tenth time in as many minutes when Ryan arrived.

Ryan Maxon had always been a handsome man. Even in his mid-forties, he still had the athletic body he'd had when I'd first met him in college. I felt a little guilty about the fact that I noticed how in shape he still was. He had a fiancé and I had Kyle, and weren't we supposed to be moving on? So instead I made myself concentrate on the gray hair at his temples, the lines at the corners of his eyes and mouth, and the shadows beneath his eyes.

I blinked.

Wait a minute. Those were some serious shadows, and the lines in his face looked deeper than the last time I'd seen him.

Ryan was a trial attorney. He'd worked long hours when we'd been married, and I was used to seeing him stressing over a hard case or a particularly difficult client. I was used to tired Ryan. I wasn't used to a Ryan who looked like he'd just lost his best friend.

I didn't feel like the world's biggest sap anymore. Maybe he really did need me.

He didn't apologize for being late. Instead he asked me if I still drank mocha lattes.

I said yes without thinking. Before I could tell him I didn't really want anything, especially anything hot, he was at the counter ordering coffee.

Well, at least that hadn't changed. He was still the same take-charge kind of guy.

He came back with two large drinks. Our fingers brushed when he handed me my latte, and I was surprised at how cold his hands were. Maybe it was just the air-conditioning, but I doubted it. Whatever was going on, Ryan was seriously upset.

Well, okay then. Time to get down to business. Ryan had always appreciated when his clients did that. I hoped he appreciated it now.

"Tell me why you called," I said before he had a chance to try to make awkward small talk.

Most people don't look me in the eye when they need to tell me something difficult. I don't take it personally. Telling secrets to a private investigator isn't easy. It's not like confessing your sins to a priest. There's no anonymity, no convenient partition to hide behind, so people tend to distract themselves in order to pretend I'm not there.

Ryan didn't do that. Whether it was his legal training—trial lawyers don't let anything intimidate them in the courtroom—or because we hadn't hidden from each other during that horrible time in our lives when Samantha had nearly died thanks to a hit-and-run driver, he looked me in the eye instead of staring down at his coffee.

"I need help with Melody," he said.

Melody was his fiancé. She was also the woman he'd left me for. While she wasn't exactly a forbidden topic, Ryan didn't mention her around me unless he had to.

"Okay," I said, drawing the word out. "What kind of help?"

"She has a stalker."

I blinked. "Aren't there laws against that kind of thing?"

"Civil and criminal."

I wasn't a cop. I also wasn't the kind of private investigator you'd find on television or in the movies. I didn't carry a gun, and I certainly didn't go around threatening men who made a habit out of harassing women.

"So what do you need me for?" I asked.

He took a sip from his cup and grimaced. I didn't think the grimace had anything to do with the taste of the coffee. "I need you to figure out who this guy is."

Wait a second. "She doesn't know who's stalking her?" Which, when I thought about it, wasn't all that strange. I dimly remembered an old television show where a stalker turned out to be a computer repairman the woman had only seen once. Things like that probably happened in real life, too.

Now Ryan glanced away. I'd hit a sore spot, and I could guess what it was.

"She knows," I said. "And she won't tell you."

"I don't know that for sure. I just have a gut feeling. I want to get a protective order issued against him. I'd like to get his ass thrown in jail, but I'll start with that. I can't do any of it if I don't know who he is. I can't seem to make her—"

He stopped himself, but I knew what he'd been about to say: *Make her understand.*

I'd heard the phrase often enough when we'd been married.

*Why can't I make you understand how important this case is? This one could make my career.*

*Why can't I make you understand I need to put in extra hours? I'm doing this for us.*

Or the one that stuck with me the most:

*Why can't I make you understand how hard this is for me?*

He'd said that the night he packed a suitcase and left my world in tatters. I'd spent a lot of time during our marriage putting Ryan and his career first because I understood how hard it was to build a career. I'd put our family first when I forgave him for his other "little" indiscretions, the ones he said didn't mean anything to him, because I understood how hard it would be on Samantha if we got divorced.

In fact, I'd spent so much time understanding him, I think he was surprised that when it came to the actual divorce, I didn't put him first. I'd put Samantha first with me a close second, and we damn well deserved it.

I took a deep mental breath. I was over all that now, right?

Right?

Water under the bridge, as my mother would say.

Well, it better be, or I shouldn't be here.

Ryan's fist, the one not holding his coffee, was clenched tight. He was trying to keep a tight rein on his emotions just like I was. I guessed he'd had more than one argument with Melody about this subject.

The last thing I wanted to do was help my ex-husband with anything to do with that woman. It was clear—at least to me— that we still had too much unresolved baggage where she was concerned. The smart thing to do would be to tell tell him thanks but no thanks, find yourself another investigator.

Then again, I've never been particularly smart where Ryan was concerned. And deep down I believed that no woman—*no* woman, no matter who she was—should have to put up with a stalker.

"Why don't you tell me what you do know?" I said.

A bit of the tension left his face. He hadn't been sure I'd say yes. That surprised me. Maybe he didn't think I was such a sap after all.

"It started out with the flowers," he said. "A single red rose delivered to her at work."

"She still work in your building?"

He gave me a look. "No. Not since we moved in together."

Melody had been the concierge at the upscale office building where Ryan had his law practice. That's how they'd met.

"She's working as a trainer at Right Track Fitness."

Of course she was.

Melody was five feet two inches of non-stop energy, someone who'd look like the former cheerleader she was until she turned eighty. I'd seen her more than once when I used to stop by Ryan's office. She'd always been pleasant to me. Once I'd found out they'd been having an affair, I'd wondered if she knew who I was all those times she'd been so cheerily pleasant or if Ryan had never bothered to tell her he was married. We'd never left his office together when she was at her desk in the building's first floor lobby.

I used to think that was a coincidence. When Ryan told me he was moving out, I realized he'd planned it that way all along.

"She said she thought I sent the rose," he said. "I didn't. Then she said it must have come from a grateful client. I didn't like the idea of some guy sending her flowers, especially since she doesn't always wear her ring while she's working, but I didn't want to make a big deal out of it. Then I found out it wasn't just one rose. It was a rose a day for a week."

"How did they show up? Floral delivery? Or from a mail-order floral delivery service?" Florists would have a record of credit card purchases. So would an online floral delivery site. If the guy had shown up at a florist's in person and paid cash, the company might have a security camera on the register and I could at least get a blurry picture of the guy.

"I asked," Ryan said. "She wouldn't tell me. Said it was just a few flowers and I was making a big deal out of nothing."

He sat for a minute without saying anything. A frown had creased his brows, and I realized something I'd never noticed before. Ryan wasn't the one with the power in his relationship with Melody.

He'd had it in ours, partly because I'd never understood why a guy like Ryan—handsome, athletic, popular—would like a girl like me. I was the one who gave in whenever Ryan wanted something. The situation was reversed in his relationship with Melody, and it made me look at him differently. Not with pity, but with something like kinship.

I'd told myself that someday I'd be able to be friends again with my ex without the hurt getting in the way. Maybe today was that day.

I took a sip of my latte and waited. It was finally cool enough to drink without scalding my tongue. Ryan had added a sprinkle of cinnamon on the top, just like I used to do myself. I hadn't had cinnamon on my lattes since he left. When I had coffee with Kyle, I had the barista add a shot of vanilla. I'd forgotten how much I liked the taste of cinnamon.

An older couple was sitting at one of the other little tables near the back. He was working on a crossword puzzle and she had her nose in a tablet reader. At first I thought they were ignoring each other until I noticed that their sandal-clad feet were rubbing up against each other beneath the table.

I missed that kind of companionship. Kyle and I weren't there yet. We might never get there, not if his daughter didn't warm up to me. His daughter was as important to him as Samantha was to me.

My mother wouldn't have approved about the way I made
Samantha the center of my life, especially after Ryan left. Kyle
had done the same thing after he and his wife split.

"It's hard to be married to a cop," he'd told me on our
second date. "The hours are lousy, my moods are lousy when a
case is going badly, and I can't always shake work by the time I
get home. And then there's always the fear that when I leave for
work, I won't be coming home."

I'd asked him if he was trying to scare me off.

"Just want you to know what you're getting yourself in for,"
he'd said.

Ryan tapped my foot with his beneath the table, startling
me. When was the last time he'd done that?

"You were always good at that," he said.

I raised an eyebrow. "Spacing out?"

"Waiting me out. It's one of the things that makes you a
good listener. You don't need to fill the silence."

It made me a good investigator, too. It was one of the things
I'd learned. Given a chance, people would tell me their stories
as long as I gave them the opportunity to talk.

Ryan seemed to be stalling, though, and that wasn't like
him. The other thing I'd learned was that sometimes people
needed a push.

"You wouldn't have asked for my help if it was just flowers,"
I said.

He nodded. "You're right. It started with flowers. Then came
the phone calls to the condo. If I answered, he'd hang up, but
not before I could hear him breathing. One call a night at first,
then two, then five or six. We had the phone number changed
—it's unlisted now—but it only took him a couple of days
before the calls started again. We have caller ID, but the
number was blocked. I was about ready to call in a couple of
favors and put a tap and trace on the line when the calls

stopped. I figured that was the end of it until she got the first picture in the mail."

He rubbed his upper lip. It was an old habit he'd picked up during the years he'd decided to try wearing a mustache and a little goatee. At the time he'd thought it made him look older, and he was under the impression juries took older attorneys more seriously. He didn't want to look like he'd just graduated law school.

The only problem was that he was constantly touching the thing. He'd rub the mustache or stroke the goatee, and that made him look more than a little like Snidely Whiplash.

When he figured out his winning record had gone downhill, he'd shaved the thing off. He'd been clean shaven ever since, but he still rubbed at his upper lip whenever he was near his emotional limits.

"Pictures of Melody, right?" I asked.

"Yeah." He took a deep breath, his gaze somewhere over my right shoulder, but I knew he was remembering the photographs. "Melody leaving work. Melody out shopping with a friend. Melody behind the wheel, waiting for a red light and talking on her cell phone. He'd printed 'bad girl, breaking the law' on that back of that picture."

Kyle had told me once that the police department had a handwriting expert they used on occasion. It was a long shot, but maybe Melody's stalker was in the system. He could have even left prints on the photographs.

"Do you still have the pictures? I've got a friend in the police department. Maybe I could—"

"She threw them out. It was another thing we fought about —destroying the evidence. Something I could have taken to the cops myself, but with no evidence..."

There was nothing the cops could do, especially if she didn't file a police report.

That's why he'd come to me.

"How's she going to feel about your ex-wife shadowing her?" I asked. "Isn't that going to make things tense for you at home?"

Not to mention tense for me.

When he looked me in the eye this time, I saw something in his gaze I hadn't seen since we thought Samantha might die: fear.

"She doesn't realize how sick some of those bastards can be. I have friends who left criminal law because they couldn't stand dealing with the clients."

I'd come face to face with two killers myself not that long ago, and they'd both been sick bastards.

"You do realize you're asking me to find someone you're afraid could be dangerous."

"You're smart, Abby. You know how to handle yourself. Melody?" He shook his head. "She's always gotten attention from men. She thinks if she ignores this guy, he'll go away. I know better, but I can't convince her."

It was the first time he'd ever compared me favorably to his fiancé. Or at least that's how I decided to take it, since an argument could also be made that he was saying I was more expendable than the new woman in his life. Look at me, trying not to be bitchy.

"All I want is a picture of the guy, a license plate number if he's driving a car," Ryan said. "Something that will help me identify him."

"How about a name? An address?"

Ryan shook his head. "A name would be great, but I don't want you tailing this guy back to wherever he lives. If he's got a car, I can track him down through DMV."

I could do that too, but I didn't mention it. If I spotted the guy driving a car, I figured I'd just use my own resources to get a name and address. Thanks to the work I was doing for Norton Greenburger, one of Reno's best criminal defense attorneys, I'd gotten pretty good at surveillance. The guy would never know I was around.

"Melody's got a morning shift at the gym tomorrow," Ryan said. "You can pick her up there."

It was my turn to shake my head. "Can't tomorrow morning. Jonathan and his mom are driving over from Nevada City so he can spend the day with Samantha."

A look of confusion passed over Ryan's face. "Jonathan?"

I realized Samantha had never told Ryan about her long-distance boyfriend. Ouch.

"A friend of hers," I said. "We've been to Nevada City to visit a few times. This is the second time they've been here."

"Jonathan," he said again, like he was trying the name on for size. "Is it serious?"

"She's sixteen. Everything's serious."

He nodded. "Think I should meet this kid?"

Jonathan was shy and kind of a nerd. I could just see how well that meeting would turn out. "She's more focused on getting ready for school than on this boy," I said. "If you want to meet him, I'll set it up, but I don't think you need to. Not right now. You've got enough on your plate."

He finished off his coffee, and this time when he spoke, he didn't look at me. "I haven't been a very good dad, have I?"

What could I say to something like that? Good was a relative term. Ryan was getting married again—and not to me—which made him the worst dad in the world according to Samantha. But he still saw her two weekends a month, called her every so often just to talk, and never missed a birthday or holiday. That made him a better dad than a lot of dads out there.

"I'll start on Monday," I said instead. "Text me the address of Melody's gym and her schedule. I'll clear my calendar."

I'd actually said "text me." Samantha would be proud. I'd

said "clear my calendar," too. I didn't know who'd be proud of me for that one. Even my mother hadn't spoken corporate.

"Thank you," he said, and I knew he meant it.

He stood up, so I did, too. He tossed his empty coffee container in the trash. I held onto mine. I still had half my latte left. I wasn't about to throw it out.

Ryan gave me a quick smile—good old frugal Abby—but I'd had a lot of practice lately trying to make ends meet. He held the door open for me as we left, both to our separate cars. I won't lie. I still felt a twinge of regret at that. We'd been married a long time.

As I left, I caught one last glimpse of the old couple sitting at the little table near the back. He was still working the crossword puzzle and she was still reading something on her tablet. I couldn't see whether they were still playing footsie, but I wanted to think they were.

Some silences between people who'd been together a long time were thick with unspoken tension and buried resentment. My own parents hadn't been that bad, but I could tell when they'd had one of their near-fights over my mother's constant criticism.

Even if I hadn't caught the foot nudge earlier, I wanted to think this couple was different. They looked like old marrieds who'd been together for fifty years and couldn't wait to get started on the next half century. I hoped they had a huge family that spent the holidays together. I imagined them going to faraway places on vacation just so they could say they'd been there.

Most of all, I hoped that tragedy had never shadowed their lives, and that the sick bastards of the world never darkened their door.

## 2

"It's gonna feel like I'm in jail, Mom."

I nodded, trying to keep my sympathetic expression in place. Not an easy task considering I'd been hearing the same complaint from Samantha throughout the summer. A very short summer from my daughter's perspective. Mine, too.

For whatever reason, the school board had decided to start school the third week in August, which seemed ridiculous to me. Nevada's a desert state, and August is the hottest month of the summer in the north.

I should know.

I got married in a church in Reno in August. The church had no air conditioning, and I could still remember standing at the altar in front of a room full of people, only about half of whom I knew, sweating up a storm in my bridal gown.

Of course, I got divorced in a cold courtroom with only the judge, my attorney, and a resident witness in attendance. I wasn't sure what was worse.

But the biggest change at school was the one Samantha was currently complaining about.

Over the summer, a chain link fence had been constructed

around her high school campus. The gates would be locked during the school day, with no one allowed in or out without authorization. Especially not anyone in my daughter's sophomore class.

Samantha was taking the whole closed-campus thing personally. Not that she'd ever left campus to go across the street to the grocery store or any of the nearby fast food places for lunch. Last year the high school cafeteria had been too new and exciting for my fresh-faced high school freshman. Apparently sophomores didn't want to eat lunch at school. It Just. Wasn't. Done.

Except now it would be, since they had no choice.

I had no idea what the juniors and seniors thought about being locked in, but the more my own high school sophomore complained about the new policy, the more I couldn't wait for school to actually start.

I blew out a breath and counted to five before I replied to Samantha's latest complaint. I was still distracted by my meeting with Ryan, and we'd just given the living room a quick once-over with the vacuum and a dust rag that used to be a dish towel in a prior life. I was still hot and sweaty, I still needed a shower, and the remains of my latte were long gone.

"What time did Jonathan say they were getting here tomorrow?" I asked Samantha in a blatant attempt to change the subject.

She rolled her eyes at me. "Around eleven. Same as when you asked last time."

This was only the second time Jonathan and his mother were driving from Nevada City so the kids could visit.

I'd blown Ryan off when he asked me if their relationships was serious, but sometimes I had to wonder. They'd become friends in an Internet chat room—not the safest of venues, which I'd discovered last December thanks to a case that had nearly cost me my life—but Jonathan seemed like a nice kid,

and I liked his mother. I'd always heard that long-distance relationships were hard to sustain, but so far my daughter and her
boyfriend seemed to be doing fine.

"Okay. Just wanted to make sure." I grinned. "You know. In
case I forgot from the zillion other times you told me."

"Please don't go senile on me, Mom. You're the only adult I
can talk to."

Good thing Ryan didn't hear that. Samantha wasn't ready to
forgive him for replacing me with Melody. I figured she'd get
there in her own time.

"Good to know," I said, and I meant it.

I'd never been able to talk to my own mother without
getting criticism in response. The last thing I wanted to do was
turn into my mother where my own daughter was concerned. I
just didn't know how to be a good single mother at the same
time I was learning how to be an independent woman who
dated.

I guess it was a good thing Kyle and I were taking it slow.

Our cat chose that moment to yell for food.

Other cats meow. Ours yelps. It's one of the reasons we keep
her dish full, but we'd been busy and must have ignored her for
too long.

Samantha giggled. "She has the best timing."

I gestured toward the guest bathroom. "Go get busy, and I'll
feed our starving cat." I gave Samantha a sideways look. Sure, I
was getting tired of the constant complaining, but I still liked
spending time with my daughter. Even if it did involve vacu-
uming and cleaning the toilet bowl. "Maybe we can squeeze in
part of a movie before I go out tonight," I said.

"Before *we* go out."

Samantha was going to her friend Maddie's house for an
end-of-the-summer party that Maddie's mother had assured
me would be chaperoned. Not that I worried about Samantha
—as far as she was concerned, Jonathan was her boyfriend and

that was that—but Maddie had developed something of a wild streak over the summer. My reputation as a "cool mom" had tarnished a bit when I'd told Samantha that Maddie couldn't come over to the house unless I was there.

"So, movie?" I asked.

Kyle and I weren't going to a movie. He didn't like to go to the movies on a Saturday night. Too many teenagers on dates. He said it made him feel old.

Whenever we did go out on a Saturday, he always took me to dinner at some restaurant I'd never heard of. Tonight we were going out for Mexican food at a family-owned place where the dad did all the cooking and his son did everything else, from bartending to waiting tables to washing the dishes. Kyle said the food was excellent, and I'd learned to trust his judgment.

Samantha wrinkled her nose. "If you shower first."

I raised my eyebrows, pretending to be offended, but I couldn't pull it off. I did need a shower. "Okay. You pick the movie while I'm in the shower."

Samantha headed off toward the guest bathroom with a plastic tote full of cleaning supplies and rubber gloves. Most kids probably hated cleaning the bathroom, but the guest bathroom didn't get a lot of traffic. It's easier to clean than the kitchen, which was next on my hit list before the shower. Samantha had taken her shower while I met with Ryan, and I was pretty sure she wouldn't be working up a sweat anytime in the near future.

The cat yelped again.

I took a look at the cat's dish. Almost full, but apparently enough was missing that the cat was worried she'd never eat again.

I filled up the little hole she'd made in her food. She sniffed at it, ate maybe one bite, and headed off toward the living room couch, content with the knowledge she wouldn't starve tonight.

"And my daughter's worried I'm going senile," I muttered.

While I wiped down the kitchen counter, I contemplated life as a spoiled housecat. Food on demand, a nice sunny spot to snooze in, and a soft lap to curl up on. Not such a bad existence.

Of course, there'd be no Samantha and no movies, and no Kyle and Mexican food and Saturday night kisses goodnight.

I still had a smile on my face when I got done with the kitchen. On my way to take a shower, I detoured through the living room and gave my confused cat a scritch beneath her chin.

"I still think I've got the better deal, cat," I told her.

## 3

Jonathan Braddock was still tall and shy and gangly, but in the eight months since Samantha and I had first met him in person, he'd filled out a little and the blemishes that had plagued his complexion were almost gone.

He would never be a heartthrob, but he had a pleasant face and warm brown eyes, and the few times he'd actually smiled without looking down at the ground, embarrassed to be noticed, he looked like the kind of kid any high school girl would be happy to go to prom with.

I'd only gotten him to smile like that a couple of times. Samantha could do it just by saying hello.

Jonathan and his mother arrived a little late, but given that the drive from Nevada City to our house in Sparks wasn't exactly a trip to the grocery store, I didn't mind. It gave me the opportunity for one last futile attempt to remove cat fur from my couch.

June Braddock, Jonathan's mother, tried to get her son to sit down in the living room and talk with the adults, but it was a lost cause. It was pretty clear the kids wanted to be off by themselves. The closest they were going to get to that was Samantha's bedroom, and only if they kept the door open. Jonathan might be shy, but he was a senior this year, and that meant he was a bundle of overactive hormones. I wasn't born yesterday. The door was going to stay open, or I'd go down to her room and open it myself.

When I made the offer, they practically bolted down the hall.

"I don't think I was ever that young," I said, staring after them.

June chuckled. She'd already fished her latest knitting project out of her tote bag and was busy doing things with needles and yarn I couldn't hope to replicate.

"I'm sad to say I remember when I was," she said. "Young, and foolish, too. Isn't that what teenagers are supposed to be?"

I'd learned a few things about June Braddock, some from her, and some from the research I'd done before I'd allowed Samantha to meet Jonathan in person. I knew she was speaking from experience.

June Tolliver had met Harry Braddock her junior year in high school. She'd had to drop out of school before graduation because she was pregnant with Jonathan's older brother.

She'd married Harry right before the baby was born, and she'd had Jonathan the year after.

Harry hadn't been prepared for life as the father of two young boys. He'd found work in a local garage repairing tires and changing oil, but the family couldn't make ends meet. They'd moved in with Harry's parents in Nevada City, a situation June had called "cramped." I could imagine.

Then Jonathan's older brother got sick. June and her husband had no insurance.

Six months after Jonathan's older brother passed away, they'd filed for bankruptcy to get out from under the medical bills.

Things had looked up for a while after that. They'd moved

into a small apartment. Harry's parents watched Jonathan during the day, and June was able to get a part-time job at a local craft store.

Then Harry left June, nearly a year to the day after their bankruptcy had been discharged.

"He just never came home one night," she'd told me. "I did all the normal things. Called the police. Called the hospitals. Called his parents and his friends."

She'd been knitting when she told me this story the last time Samantha and I had traveled to Nevada City. The needles never lost their rhythm even though June's voice had grown strained and quiet.

"One of his friends finally told me that Harry had been talking about moving to Las Vegas. Striking it rich at the tables. He thought he could be a professional gambler, you see. He used to watch all the poker shows on cable. Practiced his 'poker face' when he thought no one else was watching. It got so that Jonathan could imitate that poker face and Harry never even knew it."

She didn't have the money to hire someone like me to find him, she'd said, so she figured he would come home when he was good and ready.

Instead, she was served with divorce papers from a lawyer in Las Vegas, and two months later, she was a single mother.

It explained a lot about why she was so protective of Jonathan, and why she'd been nervous about letting him meet someone he'd talked to over the Internet. Someone from Nevada, no less.

I'd had my own reservations. People could pretend to be whoever they wanted to be on the Internet. The news was full of stories about adult men luring unsuspecting children into hookups—and worse—by pretending to be another kid online. It had taken a lot for me to overcome my natural suspicions to let Samantha meet her Internet friend.

Of course, in her case things had turned out wonderfully. Jonathan played viola, and last time he and his mother visited, the kids had filled the house with music—Samantha on piano accompanied by the rich tones from Jonathan's viola. They really did make good music together.

June's knitting needles clacked as we sat in companionable silence. She always brought some type of craft to work on during these visits.

I normally read or worked on cases while Samantha was busy doing her own thing, but I couldn't do that and just leave June sitting in my living room. The last time she'd visited, I'd put in a movie, but she hadn't watched much of it, just concentrated on her work instead, so I'd decided to leave the television off.

Of course, that left the house quieter than I was used to. If I didn't keep myself occupied, I'd nod off on the couch, something that had started happening to me more often these days, especially after nights when my insomnia kept me company. Welcome to middle age, Abby Maxon.

I'd just started planning what equipment I'd need to take tomorrow and how I'd dress for a day of stalking the stalker—anything to keep from thinking about how I'd actually be spending my day watching Ryan's fiancé; why had I agreed to this again?—when June interrupted my thoughts.

"Can I ask you a question?" she said, never looking up from her knitting.

I said sure, even though the way she asked the question made me wonder what was coming.

"Why do you do the kind of work you do?" She did glance up at me now, an almost apologetic look. "I mean, not that women can't do any kind of work they want to these days, that's not what I'm saying, but it seems like what you do is dangerous. Don't you ever worry about what would happen to your daughter if you got hurt?"

*So* not the question I was expecting.

I could have given her a flip answer. I'd certainly done that back when I'd been married and Ryan used to introduce me to his colleagues as his wife, the gumshoe.

"Most of the time, what I do isn't that dangerous," I said. "It's not like in the movies or on TV."

She grinned. "You mean you're not the female equivalent of Thomas Magnum?"

I grinned back. "Hardly. I investigate accidents for insurance defense counsel. Interview witnesses. Serve subpoenas. Those are for civil cases, and most of the time the people involved are civil, especially to me."

Her grin dimmed. "But sometimes they aren't. The first time we met, your arm was in a sling and you were all bruised up."

The week before we'd first met, I'd been kidnapped in a grocery store parking lot, thrown in the back of a panel van by a father and son who'd just killed a fifteen-year-old girl, and held captive in my own home. That case had started out as a search for a missing person.

"I don't get involved with those kinds of cases anymore," I said.

It was something I'd made clear to Norton Greenburger when I'd agreed to work part time for him. I was more than willing to track down and interview missing witnesses, but I wasn't about to investigate crimes to try to find evidence to exonerate his clients. The real perpetrators tended to take a dim view of that, which I'd learned firsthand last December.

"Good," June said. "I like you. You and your daughter, you're what I call 'good people.' I don't trust just anyone with my son, not if I'm going to let him stay for a day or two on his own."

I tried not to do a double take. So far all the kids' visits had been fully chaperoned, one-day things.

"Thanks," I said. "I think you're good people, too." I got up from the couch and picked up her empty glass to give myself a distraction. "Let me get you some more water."

I took the glass into the kitchen without waiting for a reply.

Samantha hadn't said anything about Jonathan staying with us overnight. The kids must have chatted about it online where they did most of their talking, but it would have been nice if she'd mentioned it to me.

I shot a look down the hall as I brought June's new glass of water into the living room. The door to Samantha's room was still open. I could hear murmuring voices and the occasional giggle.

My daughter was growing up. She had a boyfriend. I supposed I should be grateful that she didn't put up a fight because I wouldn't let the two of them spend time behind closed doors, but I still felt a little hurt that she hadn't mentioned the possibility of Jonathan spending more than one day here—on his own—to me.

It looked like we'd have to have a little mother-daughter chat. Not tonight. She'd be sad enough after he left, and I didn't want to go into the discussion when her emotions were already heightened.

No, I'd wait until tomorrow night. After a day of tailing Melody, I'd need a little mother-daughter time. And maybe by then I'd figure out the right way to broach the subject so we could talk about it logically.

I hoped.

# 4

By noon on Monday I'd tailed Melody to the gym, to the bank, to a juice bar that sold smoothies and wheat grass extract, to the dry cleaners, and then back to the gym. I hadn't caught sight of the man Ryan said was stalking her, and I'd begun to feel a little like a stalker myself.

When Ryan had texted me her schedule the night before, he'd also given me instructions not to let her see me. That got under my skin at first. I didn't need Ryan telling me how to do my job. I'd never told him how to run his law practice.

Then I realized why he'd given me that specific instruction.

He must not have told Melody he'd hired me to find the identity of her stalker.

Did that mean he didn't trust her?

Or did that mean she didn't want anything to do with me, so I'd be the last person she'd want following her around?

While Melody and I would never be the best of friends, I'd never been one of those ex-wives who'd put the entire blame for the breakup on the other woman. The way I saw it, it took two to tango, as the saying went, and Ryan certainly bore his share of the responsibility for that particular dance.

Not that I'm a saint. If I'd had Melody and Ryan voodoo dolls in the house immediately after Ryan left me, they would have both ended up with mysterious aches and pains and maybe a broken bone or two, and I might have slept better at night after exacting my petty revenge.

Once I'd started to cope with the idea that my marriage was over, I'd also started to come to terms with the fact that Ryan, and by extension Melody—or her future replacement because lord knows she hadn't been the only one who'd caught his eye over the years—would always be a part of my life because Ryan would always be Samantha's father. Just because we didn't get along anymore didn't mean either one of us could make unilateral decisions about the major issues involved with raising our daughter.

Or as my divorce lawyer patiently explained to me, Ryan and I would continue to have legal obligations to each other even after the divorce decree was signed. If both of us remained civil with each other and addressed those obligations like adults, we'd save ourselves a lot of grief and legal fees, not to mention spare our child any more fodder for future therapy sessions than she already had.

Melody didn't have the same obligations toward me, and I was fine if she didn't want me in her life. As long as she treated Samantha well, and according to Samantha, Melody was nice but "she's not you, Mom," I was fine not having to interact with her.

So—why had I agreed to shadow her? Possibly for days, until her stalker showed up?

Oh, yeah. That's right. Because I was trying to be friends with my ex, and he needed a friend.

In the cold light of day, now that I was actually doing the job, I wasn't so sure about the whole sap thing.

I sighed and tried to get comfortable. World's Biggest Sap was currently melting in the front seat of her car which was parked down the street from a trendy cafe on California Avenue a few blocks away from where Norton Greenburger had his office. Melody was inside the cafe having lunch.

The cafe probably had air conditioning. I'd cracked the windows in my car, but I was still sweltering.

She'd gone in the cafe alone, and I couldn't see through the cafe's front windows, so I had no clue who she was having lunch with. She could have made my job a little easier if she'd decided to eat at one of the little two-person tables on the sidewalk in front of the cafe, but then again, she might have spotted me just sitting in my car. I'd take what I could get.

I settled in for the wait with a peanut butter and jelly sandwich I'd brown bagged that morning.

Forty-five minutes later she came out the front door and headed toward the little parking lot on the side of the cafe. She was still alone, which seemed odd to me. If she'd met someone for lunch, wouldn't they have all come out together?

Less than a minute after Melody left the cafe, a man walked out. Like Melody, he was alone. He wouldn't have caught my attention except for the fact that he didn't immediately head toward the parking lot or down the street in the opposite direction, like he was heading toward a car parked on the street.

No, this man just stood on the sidewalk in front of the cafe.

I wasn't the only one who must have thought that was weird. An older guy sitting alone at one of the outside tables looked up from his tablet and frowned. He'd been eating his lunch in solitary silence, alone with whatever was on his tablet. I hoped it was a good book. I read a lot myself, but so far I stuck to books of the dead tree variety.

The man who'd disturbed Reader Guy's lunch had a cell phone in one hand. While he might have looked like he was checking messages, it was clear, even from my vantage point, that he was faking it.

What he was really doing was watching Melody.

Hello, stalker suspect.

I grabbed my camera. It's a small digital model, but it's got a built-in zoom that makes the clunky zoom lens on my ancient 35mm camera look like the Hubbell telescope in comparison. I steadied the camera on my steering wheel and zoomed in on the guy, and he jumped into high definition on the display on the back of the camera.

He was tall and trim with an athletic build—sturdy shoulders, narrow waist, lean legs. He had dark hair cut moderately short in a style that made me think lawyer or banker, and he was wearing a conservative dark suit that could have put him squarely in either profession.

I estimated his age at somewhere in his thirties—the little screen could only show me limited details, so I'd have to enlarge the pictures on my computer later if I wanted to check for crow's feet or fine lines around his eyes and mouth. He was clean shaven and wore his tie snugged up tight even though the temperature outside was in the middle nineties.

I clicked off a few pictures while he stood on the sidewalk outside the cafe staring after Melody. He could just be a horny guy who'd decided to check out the hot chick—Melody had gone to the cafe wearing an oversized tunic over slinky salmon-colored tights that left nothing to the imagination—but I didn't think so. Something about this guy's posture said his interest wasn't casual.

Was this Melody's stalker?

Would a stalker be that bold? I'd had a mental image of a guy lurking in shadows or hiding in his car, like I was, and conducting discrete surveillance of his subject. Not somebody standing out in the open checking her out like a guy at a singles' club.

I kept clicking off pictures, hoping that the guy would turn around and give me a few full face shots.

Out of the corner of my eye, I saw Melody drive her brand

new Volkswagen Beetle out of the parking lot and onto California Avenue. She'd be driving right past me, but as long as I stayed still in my car, chances were she wouldn't see me. From what I'd observed so far from tailing her, Melody was fairly oblivious to her surroundings while she was driving.

I was so busy concentrating on the guy on the sidewalk who'd turned to watch Melody drive away that I almost didn't see another car pull away from the curb and into traffic directly behind Melody's car.

The second car was a white SUV, a smaller model with tinted windows—what car salesmen liked to call "soccer mom" cars—and it had been parked on the street almost right in front of the cafe's parking lot along with a bunch of other similar cars crowded against the curb.

I hadn't seen anyone get in the SUV. I would have noticed. Which meant that whoever was in that car, they'd been sitting inside the car at least as long as I'd been sitting in mine.

Someone else doing surveillance?

I refocused the camera and managed to click off a couple of quick shots of the white SUV as it drove past me, now a couple of car lengths behind Melody's car. The sun glinted off the windshield at precisely the wrong angle. I'd hoped to at least get an impression of whether the driver was a man or woman, but I couldn't tell. At least I thought I'd gotten a shot of the license plate.

The whole thing with the SUV could have been a coincidence, but it didn't feel like it. That car had been waiting for Melody.

Had I seen it earlier today and not realized it? I had no idea. It seemed like everyone in the city drove an SUV, and a majority of the SUVs were white. Nothing I'd spotted on this one made it stand out from any other white SUV on the road.

Then there was the guy outside the cafe. He'd hung around

just to stare at Melody while he pretended to look at something on his cell phone.

Or was he taking pictures of her with his cell? The newer cell phones could take camera quality photographs. I'd taken some of my own for Norton Greenburger.

After a morning of nothing, I suddenly had two potential stalkers. The white SUV had been heading west on California. The guy on foot outside the restaurant was heading toward the same parking lot where Melody had parked her car. I couldn't tail them both, so I had to decide which one to follow.

Based on the schedule Ryan had provided, I knew Melody was working at the gym that afternoon. She coached spin classes at one-thirty and three, and wouldn't be leaving again until at least four. If the SUV was tailing her, I knew where it would be. With any luck, I already had a license plate number, and if I didn't, I could grab it later in the afternoon.

The man on foot, on the other hand—I had nothing but his picture. No name. No license plate number. No fingerprint or DNA or even shoe size.

I needed something else.

I put my car in gear and drove toward the parking lot.

# 5

The man who'd been standing on the sidewalk staring at Melody didn't get into a car in the parking lot next to the cafe. Instead he cut through the lot on foot and kept walking down Hill Street toward downtown.

Following a pedestrian with a car is no easy feat. Unless I wanted to piss off every driver behind me by coasting along at fifteen miles per hour, I couldn't just tail the guy, and even if I did, all the blaring horns would blow the whole stealth aspect of the job.

Nor could I just keep circling the block again and again. If he went into one of the many old houses that had been converted into offices that crowded the side streets in this part of Reno while I was on the other side of the block, I'd be screwed.

I had to improvise. Luckily, I'd gotten good at this part of the job thanks to years of waiting out reluctant witnesses who didn't want to be served with the subpoena or the summons they were trying to duck.

The parking spots along both sides of Hill Street were crammed with cars, but there was an empty loading zone near the back of a two-story mansion that had been converted into office suites.

I pulled into the loading zone, switched on my car's hazard lights, and picked up a clipboard I'd stashed in the pocket behind the passenger seat. I pretended to look through the documents I kept on the clipboard—a phony but authentic-looking subpoena complete with notes on where to find a non-existent witness—while I kept one eye on Mr. Not So Subtle.

He crossed the street in the middle of the block, and then cut across another parking lot, this one behind the Nevada Museum of Art. When he got through the parking lot, he headed east on Liberty Street, still on foot.

I could barely see him now, so I pulled back into traffic. I got to the corner of Hill and Liberty just in time to see him go into one of the many bank buildings near the intersection of Liberty and Virginia Streets.

I swore under my breath. This particular building had at least ten stories full of offices. I should have gotten out of my car and followed the guy on foot. Even though he'd been walking at a pretty good clip, I might have been able to follow him closely enough to tell whether he took the elevator, and if so, to which floor.

I did have one advantage, though. I had his picture on my camera.

I parked in a space in the building's attached garage earmarked for bank customers. Before I got out of my car, I brought up the clearest picture I'd taken of the guy on my camera's display screen and then took a picture of the picture with my cell phone. The end result wasn't perfect, but at least now it looked like something I'd snapped with my cell.

I took a twenty dollar bill out of my wallet and shoved it in the pocket of my jeans, and I was ready to go.

This building had a security guard instead of a concierge. The lobby where he sat was a vast open area with no locked gates or metal detectors, so I wasn't quite sure what the elderly Hispanic security guard was supposed to secure. The entrance to the bank was at the other end of the lobby from where he sat behind a built-in desk. I doubted he could get to the bank in time do to anything constructive if robbers hit the place.

Maybe his real purpose was to help lost souls. If that was the case, he was just the person I was looking for. Next to the man I was really there to find, that is.

I put on my best "trust me" expression and headed toward the guard desk.

He looked up from his own clipboard, and I smiled at him. He didn't exactly smile back, but he didn't look like he wanted to shoot me, either.

"Hi," I said. "I wonder if you could help me."

"I'll do my best," he said. He had a faint accent, not exactly south of the border but definitely not a local.

"This is kind of silly, and maybe I'm being too honest, but I was having lunch at that cafe on California—you know the one all the lawyers go to?"

His expression said he knew where I meant but it wasn't someplace he cared to go.

"Well, this guy dropped twenty dollars on the sidewalk." I pulled the twenty out of my pocket. "I yelled at him, but I guess he didn't hear me. He just took off down the sidewalk. I tried to catch him, but his legs are longer than mine. Plus, I'm not in really great shape."

I smiled again, this one a "what can I say?" type smile, and this time the guard smiled back. He had a few extra pounds around his middle himself.

"I saw him come in here," I said. "Maybe you could help me figure out who he is so I can give him his money back?"

"I dunno," he said. "A lot of people come in here. If you're gonna describe him to me, I hope he's got a missing arm or a flashy earring or some interesting tattoos. White guy in a suit would be most of the guys in this building."

"I can do better." I pulled my cell from my pocket. "I have a picture."

Now he looked at me like I was nuts. "You took his picture?"

I shrugged. "I was about to take a picture of myself outside the restaurant—a selfie, right?" Samantha had taught me that term. Up until this moment I'd never actually said "selfie" before. "I had the camera on. I never even thought twice, just snapped his picture."

I turned my phone around so the guard could see the picture of Mr. Not So Subtle. It wasn't the best picture. I'd deliberately chosen one I'd taken by accident when I'd tried to get a picture of the white SUV. In the shot, the guy was clearly walking away from my position.

The guard gave me a long look. "Lady, if you're just trying to meet this guy, I have to give you credit for coming up with the craziest story I've ever heard. If you're not, if you really just want to give this guy his money back, I'm not sure that means you're still not crazy."

I tried to look sane and non-threatening. Sweat was running down my back and freezing on my forehead. The building didn't skimp on air conditioning.

"Twenty bucks is twenty bucks," I said. "I know I'd want it back if I'd dropped it."

Twenty bucks was important money to the security guard, too. I could see it in his expression, and I wondered if I would have gotten an answer quicker if I'd just given him the money in exchange for the information.

Finally, he shrugged. "That looks like the new banker. I don't know his name, but I see him sitting at one of those desks in the back."

I gave the guard a brilliant smile. "Thank you!"

He shook his head at me. "There are easier ways of getting a date, you know. You're pretty good looking."

*For a woman your age.* He didn't say it, but I heard it just the same.

I decided to take the compliment and not react to the subtext.

"Wish me luck!" I said, and headed off to the bank.

---

THE LAST THING I would want was a date with Mr. Not So Subtle, even if I wasn't already dating someone I liked a great deal.

The guy in the picture was seated behind the last desk in a row of cookie-cutter cherry wood desks off to the left of the teller windows. The desks were large and meant to be impressive. It might have worked if the first three desks in the row weren't obviously vacant.

Banking had fallen on hard times, and like all businesses that needed to cut expenses, extraneous staff were the first to go. Mr. Not So Subtle had either survived the cuts by being good at his job or by accepting a new position at a different branch. I suspected the latter since he didn't have a name plate on his desk.

He did, however, have a stack of business cards on his desk. To get a name to go with the pictures on my camera, I'd have to actually talk to the guy. Ryan would have a fit if he found out.

Well, that meant I'd just have to make sure Ryan never found out, even if I lost my twenty bucks in the process.

Mr. Not So Subtle didn't have anyone in the two clients chairs in front of his desk, so I put a pleasant smile on my face and walked up to him, all the while reminding myself that if he was the stalker, he could be a dangerous guy beneath his conservative suit and haircut.

"Hi," I said.

He looked up at me from whatever he'd been doing on his computer and smiled his own version of a professional smile. "What can I help you with?" he said.

His voice was pleasant, mid-range for a man and without any discernible accent. Up close, I could see fine lines around his eyes and at the corners of his mouth, and I amended my earlier assessment of his age. He could be a well-preserved forty-five or a stressed-out thirty-five, but I'd bet he'd long since kissed his twenties goodbye.

He didn't have a wedding ring on his left hand. In fact, he wasn't wearing any jewelry at all, and it didn't look like either of his ears had ever been pierced.

"You didn't happen to drop a twenty dollar bill on the side-walk, did you?" I said, keeping to the story I'd told the security guard, just in case the guard decided to mention the crazy lady and her crazy story to anyone else.

Plus, since I knew damn well he hadn't, his response would give me an idea just how honest the guy was. I deliberately omitted the name of the street. I didn't want him to think I was stalking him. Irony much?

He raised one eyebrow. "A twenty dollar bill?"

I pulled the twenty back out of my pocket. "Is it yours?"

He actually pulled out his wallet to check.

From where I was standing, I could see a small wad of cash in his billfold, along with bunch of credit cards.

He rifled through the cash, and then shook his head. "Nope. Not me." He flashed me a friendlier smile. "Are you sure you're real? Most people would have just pocketed the money."

I did exactly that, stuffing my twenty dollars back in my jeans.

"Frugal, but honest. That's me." I glanced down at a stack of brochures I'd noticed on his desk. "You don't have any good deals on a checking account for a frugal but honest person, do you?"

He handed me a brochure and started in on his banker spiel, rattling off minimum deposits, monthly fees, and premium services faster than I could have followed even if I wanted to open a new account at his bank, which I didn't. All I wanted was his business card so I could get out of there.

Inspiration struck. I held up a finger, the universal sign for "just a minute," and fished my cell phone out of my purse. I kept the face of the phone turned towards me as I looked at it.

"Damn," I said, staring at the phone before I put it back in my purse. "Reminder," I said to him. "I have an appointment in fifteen minutes, and if I don't head out now, I'm going to be late." I picked up one of the brochures off his desk. "Mind if I take this?"

"Not a bit." He handed me a business card. "Give me a call when you decide what account's right for you, and I'll get you all set up."

I glanced at the name on the card—Justin Sewell. No title beneath his name, just a slogan beneath the bank's name: *Let me be your personal banker!*

Not likely.

I thanked him and left before he could ask for my name.

It wasn't until I was halfway to my car that I realized Justin worked for the same bank that Melody had visited that morning. Different branch, but it was the same bank.

Reno was still a small town even with the growth spurt that had seen the town expand to fill the valley and creep into the foothills—growth that had slowed to a trickle with the housing bust—and I was used to running into people I hadn't thought about in years, much less seen around town. Still, the fact that Justin Sewell, aka Mr. Not So Subtle, worked at the bank Melody frequented could have explained how he'd seen her in the first place. People didn't always do their banking at the same branch. Sometimes they used whatever branch was more convenient at the time.

Stalkers fixated on their prey for any number of reasons that made no sense to the rest of us. Melody could have been nice to Sewell one day, said a simple "thank you" that meant nothing to her but became the connection he wove an elaborate relationship around, like a spider creating a web.

I tucked Justin Sewell's business card in my pocket next to my twenty dollars. I'd do a quick background check on him when I got home and had access to my computer again. Samantha told me I could do almost any kind of internet search on my smart phone, but my eyes liked looking at a bigger screen.

Except for the way he'd gazed after Melody when she'd left the cafe, Justin Sewell didn't strike me as a dangerous man, but what did a stalker look like? Certainly not like the bad guy in that TV show I'd seen years ago. He'd been creepy and sweaty and obviously unhinged. I doubted stalkers in real life were that easy to spot. But had I caught anything on camera other than a healthy—if in poor taste—interest by a single man for a good-looking woman?

I didn't know. That wasn't my call, really. I'd give Ryan the man's name, copies of the photos I'd taken, and a report that detailed what I saw and anything of interest I learned from the background check.

In the meantime, I needed to catch up with Melody at the gym. My day of following her wasn't over yet.

My day, and maybe whoever was driving that white SUV.

## 6

I'd just passed the intersection of California and Arlington, heading west on California, when the theme song from *Pirates of the Caribbean* interrupted my thoughts.

Norton Greenburger had insisted I join the twenty-first century and get a smart phone, so I'd upgraded my old flip phone for a new model that had more apps than I'd ever use.

My new cell also had programmable ringtones. Samantha had gone crazy uploading specialized ringtones for me. Kyle's was the theme from *Pirates of the Caribbean* since the first time we'd met he'd been using a *Pirates* notepad his daughter had given him.

I had to admit—every time I heard that ringtone, my heart gave a little extra beat.

I grinned and fished my phone out of my purse. I answered the call on speaker.

"Hey," I said. "What's up?"

"Are you breaking the law again?" Kyle Beacham asked.

Driving and talking on the phone was illegal in Nevada now unless the driver used a hands-free device. I had a Bluetooth gadget with an earpiece and a microphone, but the earpiece was sitting on my office desk with a dead battery since I'd lost the charger. I hadn't been motivated enough to order a replacement. I'd never much liked the thing in the first place.

"You're on speaker, Detective," I said, as if he couldn't tell. "So watch what you say."

He chuckled. "I'll try not to say anything scandalous." I heard a chair scrape in the background. He must have been working at his desk. He wouldn't say anything scandalous at work. One thing I'd learned early about Kyle Beacham—he's a dedicated, no nonsense cop. The only reason he was calling me from work was because he had a minute between tasks. "So how goes the surveillance?"

"Promising," I said.

I didn't give him details and he didn't ask. I'd told him about the basic job during dinner Saturday night.

Over shredded-beef enchiladas that were to die for, we'd discussed stalkers in general. In Kyle's opinion, the truly obsessed stalkers were only one step removed from rapists, and that made them dangerous, especially when crossed. Like Ryan, he'd advised me to keep my distance. If I inserted myself between Melody and whoever was stalking her, I'd be putting myself in harm's way if the stalker felt threatened.

When I'd mentioned that Ryan just wanted enough information to get a protective order against the guy, Ryan nodded. "With some guys, a TPO serves as a wake-up call that what they're doing carries serious consequences. With other guys?" He shrugged. "It's about as effective as a paper bullet. Words with no real sting."

Of course, as Kyle had explained to me, protective orders came in two flavors—temporary and extended. The penalty for violating an extended protective order did have a serious sting —a felony charge and jail time. I'd told Kyle I hoped it didn't come down to that.

Kyle had offered to talk to Melody, off the clock, or have a female officer talk to her. I'd told him I'd pass the offer along to Ryan. I still planned on doing just that, but since it had become clear that Ryan was keeping my surveillance job a secret, I doubted Ryan would mention the offer to Melody.

As I talked to Kyle on the phone—legally—I took the gentle curve from California to Mayberry, heading toward McCarran Boulevard. The stately homes that bordered California Avenue gave way to middle class subdivisions that had a good thirty or forty years on them. McCarran marked the border between those middle class subdivisions and the high-end houses in Caughlin Ranch.

Back when I'd been married to Ryan and we went to parties with other attorneys and their wives, Caughlin Ranch had been *the* place to live for young, upwardly-mobile professionals. As far as I was concerned, those upwardly-mobile professionals could keep their expensive, cookie-cutter homes. The houses were nestled in the low foothills to the west of town, but those foothills were covered with sagebrush and cheat grass and were magnets for summer wildfires.

The gym where Melody worked catered to the middle and upper middle class residents of this part of town. Located in a little shopping center off West McCarran that also housed a dentist's office, a gas station, and a pizza parlor, the gym boasted that it had the newest technology when it came to exercise equipment, as well as its own juice bar and spa.

I wondered if the gym got any business from people who'd felt guilty about over-indulging in their favorite pizza, or if pizza was the reward for people who'd just sweated off five pounds of water weight in one of her spinning classes.

Come to think of it, I wondered why Melody had gone to another juice bar that morning when she could have had a smoothie without leaving work. Maybe she'd wanted a hot pretzel smothered in cheese sauce to go along with her healthy drink and didn't want anyone at the gym to know. That kind of sneaking around might almost make me like her.

Almost.

"So tell me," Kyle said. "Do you like saxophone music?"

Uh oh.

Kyle's daughter Lauren had turned twelve in June. She was smart as a whip and had the same kind of single-minded determination that made her dad an outstanding cop.

The year before, her mother had enrolled Lauren in a band program where she learned how to play clarinet. She'd enjoyed it so much she wanted to learn as many woodwind instruments as she could. She'd signed up for the band program at the middle school where she'd be starting—a week from today—but she also wanted to play in jazz band. Not clarinet. She wanted to play saxophone, and she'd taught herself the basics.

Kyle had signed her up for three summer school classes: a beginning class where she played saxophone, an intermediate class where she played clarinet with kids a couple years older than she was, and a jazz band class where she was the lowest chair in the saxophone section. Kyle had to get special permission to enroll her in the intermediate and jazz band classes, but Lauren had passed both auditions with flying colors.

Of course, that didn't mean she thought she was prepared enough for the audition she'd have to pass to get on jazz band as a new seventh grader. According to Kyle, she'd been practicing almost constantly.

"I love her, but she's driving me nuts." Even though his voice was distorted by the cell phone's speaker, I could hear the sharp edge frustration put on his words. "How do you handle it when Samantha plays the same section of music over and over again?"

Ryan and I had started Samantha on piano lessons when she'd been little. She wasn't a prodigy by any means, but she enjoyed it enough that practicing wasn't a chore.

These days she played mostly classical tunes. She was an excellent sight reader, and unless the sheet music was too complex, she could play pretty much anything just by reading the music. She still practiced though, playing the same few bars over and over, especially if the fingering was tricky, so I knew exactly what Kyle meant.

"I learned to tune it out," I said. "Bury my nose in a book. Put on a set of headphones, the kind that covers my ears, not those little earbuds."

"And that works?"

"Most of the time. Unless she's angry, then she really pounds the keys." Samanatha's anger music was a difficult classical piece with a lot of bass notes. I could hear that stuff through walls. It was a wonder the neighbors didn't complain. "I have noise canceling headphones."

"Noise canceling headphones." Kyle repeated the words slowly, like he was writing the information down in a notebook. He'd filled up the little *Pirates of the Caribbean* notebook he'd had when we first met long ago. The last notebook I'd seen him pull out of his pocket had Katniss from *The Hunger Games* on the cover.

By the time I pulled into the parking lot for Melody's gym, we'd progressed from talking about our kids to discussing current movies and which ones I might like to see. Kyle had pretty eclectic tastes in movies, although most cop movies made him cringe, they were so unrealistic.

I spotted Melody's car parked off to the side of the gym near one of the spindly trees that dotted the shopping center's parking lot.

At least she was where she was supposed to be. Now I needed to check for white SUVs.

I counted no less than five of the things in the parking lot. Three of them had no tinting on the windows, so I could rule them out. Of the two with tinted windows, one had a crease in the front bumper on the driver's side. I didn't remember seeing anything like that on the SUV that had followed Melody from the cafe.

I parked a row away from the remaining white SUV. It had Nevada plates. I jotted down the number.

Kyle was still on the phone, which surprised me. We must have been talking for nearly fifteen minutes. "Slow day?" I asked.

"I am currently without a major crime wave, thank god, and hanging around the station waiting to conduct an interview. My witness is late."

I felt bad for the witness. Kyle was a punctual man. He didn't appreciate tardiness in others. I'd been late for a date only once, and it had put a strain on the evening. Whenever Kyle was running late, it always had something to do with his job, and he always called.

"Think you can run a plate for me?" I asked.

"Part of your surveillance?"

"Yeah." I gave him the make and model of the SUV and the license plate number. "I caught this car following Melody. Tinted windows, so I can't see inside."

I heard him clicking keys. I didn't ask him very often to get information for me that I couldn't get myself, or that I couldn't get as quickly as he could.

While I sat waiting for the information from Kyle, I got a funny feeling down my spine. It almost felt like I was being watched. Which I might have been if someone was sitting inside the white SUV studying me like I was studying him. Or her.

"White SUV, you say?" Kyle asked.

I confirmed the color, and gave Kyle the make and model. "Don't ask me what year," I said. "All I can tell is that it's newer, not new, but not real old either."

He was quiet for a moment, probably studying the readout on his screen.

"Something odd's going on," he finally said. "I know you're doing this as a favor for your ex, but I'd feel better if you turned the case over to someone else. The sooner the better."

I blinked. "I'm not going to get in a confrontation with the guy. I just need a name to give Ryan, and he can take it from there. The last thing I want is to put myself on some crazy's radar."

"You might already be in over your head."

What?

"That white SUV," Kyle said. "It belongs to a cop."

## 7

The last thing I expected to hear was that the white SUV that had followed Melody from the cafe on California Avenue to her gym on West McCarran belonged to an undercover cop.

"Lewis Richards," Kyle said. "I busted him once for possession with intent."

"You arrested another cop?" I asked.

"I didn't know he was a cop at the time."

Kyle explained that the bust had happened when he was still a patrol cop. He and his partner had responded to a call about a woman being harassed in a local park. They'd arrived at the park to find the woman long gone and instead stumbled into a drug deal going down.

Richards had been one of two adults in the park holding a reasonable amount of illegal drugs. The teenagers they'd been selling to faded away into the night, and the adults tried to flee on foot. Kyle and his partner had chased them down.

"We got him back to the station, put him in an interrogation room by himself, and he told us he was a cop and to check with his captain. Long story short, his captain called our captain, and Richards walked after spending the night in a cell. The word came down that we weren't to bust the guy again unless we got orders from higher up the food chain."

I stared at the white SUV. It didn't look like the kind of car that belonged to an undercover cop. Then again, what I knew about undercover cops came from TV shows and movies.

If Kyle had still been a patrol cop when he'd busted Richards, that would have been more than five years ago since I knew that's how long Kyle had been a detective. A lot of things could change in five years.

"Is he still working undercover?" I asked.

I could almost hear Kyle's shrug. "I saw him a few times on the street after that, but I haven't heard a word about him in years, official or unofficial."

"Any way you can find out?"

This time the momentary silence on the other end of the phone had a chill to it. "I thought all you wanted was a name, then you were off the case."

That had been before I knew someone who'd been involved in the drug scene was following my ex's fiancé. This woman was a part of my daughter's life. If she had anything to do with illegal drugs, anything at all that would make an undercover cop interested, I wanted to know.

"What would you do if an undercover drug cop was following your ex's new boyfriend?" I asked.

"That's different. I'm a cop. You're—"

"Not," I finished. "I know. I also know my limits, but I can't just walk away from this. Are you going to help me?"

His sigh was audible over the speaker. "I'll see what I can find out about Richards. Just promise me you'll stay safe."

I knew he was worried about me. I'd given him good cause to be worried.

Kyle had been one of the cops who'd broken into my home last December and found me, battered and with a dislocated shoulder, fending off a killer in my own bedroom with only a can of pepper spray. The last thing I wanted was a repeat performance of something like that.

"I'll stay safe," I said.

---

I STAYED in my car for another fifteen minutes after Kyle's witness arrived and he had to get off the phone. I spent that time warring with myself about what to do.

Technically, Kyle was right. I only had to get the names of the man—or men—stalking Melody. I already had two names, plus I had a business card for Justin Sewell and more information than that on Lewis Richards.

If it was Richards driving the SUV.

Just because the car belonged to him didn't mean he was driving it. Would an undercover cop loan his car to some druggie he was in a gang with? Or was he married, and this was his wife's car? I'd never actually seen the person driving the car. All I really had to give Ryan was the license plate and the name of the registered owner of the car.

What kind of an investigator would I be if I didn't get him the information he really needed?

Then there was the question of what to do about Melody.

If it turned out it really was the cop following her, there had to be a reason. Would a cop, especially a cop who wanted to keep a low, undercover profile, do something as stupid as stalking?

Okay, yeah, surveillance work was technically stalking, but I didn't think buying flowers for the target of the surveillance was exactly in the How To Be A Good Undercover Cop handbook.

So if the cop hadn't sent her the flowers or the pictures, if he wasn't the guy calling at all hours, that left Justin Sewell, Mr. Not So Subtle, as potential creepy stalker guy, and the cop as just a guy doing his job.

Which, if he was a good undercover cop, meant he might have his own pictures of creepy stalker guy doing his thing.

The first thing for me to do was figure out a way to find out if Lewis Richards had been driving the SUV. I hadn't seen any movement in the SUV since I'd been here, but that didn't mean anything. I couldn't tell through the tinted windows if anyone was even in the SUV.

I grabbed my purse and my sunglasses. I'd stashed my camera in my purse, but I didn't need a camera for this part of the job.

The SUV was parked a row over from my car in a space in between me and the entrance to the gym. I cut through the parked cars, angling through the lot so that I'd walk next to the passenger side of the SUV. It was a bright, sunny afternoon, and with the angle the SUV was parked, the sun shining on the driver's side would show me a silhouette of anyone sitting inside the SUV, even if I couldn't make out a face through the tinted windows.

When I got close to the front of the SUV, I stopped and dug through my purse for my cell phone. Nobody had called me, but anyone in the SUV wouldn't know that.

I held my cell up to my ear and pretended to have a short conversation. The pretend conversation gave me an excuse to pause for a moment before walking by the side of the SUV.

I needn't have bothered with the charade. Unless they were stretched out flat on the floorboards, there was no one inside.

Damn. Now what?

I put my cell back in my purse. If anyone was watching, I'd look suspicious if I just turned around and went back to my car, and then sat inside without leaving.

It looked like it was time for me to get closer to the woman whose watcher I was supposed to be watching. Maybe it would give me a chance to see what the hell she was up to.

It was time for me to go to the gym.

## 8

Right Track Fitness wasn't like any gym I'd ever been in.

Not that I'd been in a lot, but over the years I'd served a few subpoenas on bodybuilder types, and it was always easier to track them down at the gym. Those places had been little more than a huge room filled with exercise machines and weight benches surrounded by mirrored walls where sweaty guys focused on the reflections of their bulging muscles and strained expressions while chanting the kind of affirmations I wouldn't want my daughter to hear.

When I walked through the front doors of Melody's gym, I thought I was in an upscale beauty salon and day spa.

None of the workout areas were visible from the spacious foyer. A wall faced with river rock rose two stories behind a gently curving reception counter that would have dwarfed my living room. Decorator candles burned low in groupings of three arranged in tasteful spots along the gleaming black granite countertop. Lush green plants softened the hard-edged look of the counter and gave the room a forest glade feel. A fountain burbled off to one side, and New Age music played low in the background. Light came from globes hanging on long chains from the ceiling, but it was subdued lighting.

Put a recliner in the middle of this room, give me a good book to read, and I'd be a happy camper.

A woman who looked like she'd stepped out of a fashion magazine stood off to one side behind all that gleaming black granite. She smiled a professional smile when I walked in.

"Can I help you?" she asked.

I smiled back. "I'm not sure I have the right place," I said. "But there's a car in the parking lot with its lights on. If it belongs to one of your members, I wouldn't want them to get done with their workout only to find a dead battery."

The woman's smile dimmed just a fraction. "Someone actually left their lights on?"

I didn't blame her for being skeptical. There wasn't a cloud in the sky, but the headlights story was the best idea I could come up with. There was no way this woman would mistake me for someone who worked out at the gym, or even someone who'd want a day pass just to give the gym a try. I wasn't out of shape exactly, but I got most of my exercise doing housework.

"I know," I said. "It seems silly to me, too, but maybe they were on the freeway and just forgot to turn them off when they got to town."

I-80 was only a couple of blocks away. It was feasible, right? Lots of people I knew drove with their headlights on whenever they got on the freeway, night or day.

"Ah. You're right," the woman said. "I suppose I can have the instructors ask around. Did you get the license plate number?"

I handed her the information for the white SUV I'd jotted down on a scrap of paper out in the parking lot. "Hope you find whoever it is," I said.

A door at the far side of the room opened about the same time I turned away from the front counter. Another fashion-model thin woman walked through, this one with a thin sheen of sweat on her face and a towel draped over one shoulder. She wore a black Lycra workout suit with hot pink accents that fit like a second skin and left pretty much nothing to the imagination.

For a moment I thought Ms. Lycra was Melody and I figured I was busted, but then I realized I was hearing Melody's voice through the open doorway.

I glanced that way just in time to see her engaged in a rather intense conversation with a man in a white tank top and shoulder-length dirty-blond hair. I couldn't see his face, but I caught enough of a look to know that the guy was no stranger to some sort of workout routine. His shoulder muscles weren't exactly bulging, but he wasn't a ninety-pound weakling either.

I shouldn't have lingered, but I'm curious by nature. Norton Greenburger says that's what makes me such a good investigator. In another era, I might have been the neighborhood busybody. This particular investigation had taken an unexpected turn, and I wanted to find out as much as I could about Melody. So I stayed a moment too long, trying to listen in on what she and this man were talking about, and she spotted me.

Crap.

Well, the best defense is a good offense.

"Hi!" I said, summoning up my best smile. "I didn't realize you worked out here."

She gave an annoyed glance at the man, then put on a smile as fake as my own and followed Ms. Lycra into the foyer. The guy followed along, hanging back a few steps.

"I work here," she said. "Thinking about joining? I think we have a special right now for new members, don't we, Stacy?"

The fashion model I'd given the license plate number to shot Melody a surprised look, then recovered enough to smile at me. "We do," she said. "But—"

"I wasn't thinking of joining," I said. "I stopped off for gas and noticed someone had left their lights on in the parking lot."

Stacy held up my note. "She thought it might be one of our guests."

Melody gave me a look that said she didn't believe me for a minute, but she took the note from Stacy. The note where I'd jotted the make, model, and color of the SUV along with the license plate.

"Oh, look," Melody said to the guy in the white tank top and the well-defined muscles. "Isn't this your car?"

Now that I had a good look at his face, I could see that Mr. Muscles was somewhere in his late thirties. He had a neat little beard the same color as his dirty-blond hair, and the edge of a tattoo peeked out from beneath the front of his tank top. He had more tribal tattoos wrapped around his upper arms.

He might have been a handsome man at one time, but his face had a hard look, and it wasn't just because he'd burned off all except maybe one percent of his body fat. I'd seen guys like him in every gym I'd ever been in, the guys who took body sculpture to a whole new level. His muscles might not be bulging, but he was just as serious as a Mr. Universe about keeping in shape. Could he possibly still be an undercover drug cop?

Mr. Muscles looked at the note Melody still held, and then at me. His expression said he didn't believe me either.

"Yeah," he said. "My car. Imagine that."

For a minute the three of us stood there not moving, then Mr. Muscles grumbled about needing his keys, and he disappeared through the door to the back.

"Well, great!" I said to no one in particular. "I'm glad that all worked out."

Behind the desk, Stacy looked confused, like she knew something important had just happened, but she had no idea what. She shared a look with Ms. Lycra, who shrugged her shoulders.

It was time for me to leave. I'd done enough damage. I

didn't have a name for the SUV's driver, but at least I had a pretty good physical description. I could give that to Kyle, and he should be able to tell me whether Mr. Muscles was Lewis Richards.

"Tell Ryan hello for me," I said to Melody.

She gave me a brittle smile in response. "One of many things I'll be telling him."

I was sure of that.

I beat feet out of the gym. I'd taken maybe half a dozen steps when I heard the door open behind me.

"Want to tell me what that was all about?"

Any semblance of a fake smile had left Melody's face.

"I don't know what you mean," I said.

"You're not a very good liar."

Not something a private investigator wants to hear. I sighed. "Look, I'm here doing a job. It has nothing to do with you."

"Sure, it doesn't." She had her arms folded across her ample chest. "Does Ryan have you checking up on me? Following me?"

I could have pretended to be surprised that she'd even suspect Ryan would hire me to follow her, but genuine surprise was a hard emotion to fake and she probably wouldn't have believed me anyway. Time to go back on the offensive.

"Why?" I asked. "Is there some reason he should hire a private detective to follow you around?" I crossed my own arms in front of my less than ample chest. "Are you keeping something from him?"

Her lips pressed into a thin line. "None of your business," she said from between clenched teeth.

I'd hit a nerve, and that made me curious. I had to remind myself that it wasn't my job to investigate her. Standing out in front of the gym arguing wouldn't get me anywhere, and she was right. It wasn't any of my business.

"Look, if I upset you, I'm sorry." I shrugged. "I'm on a job, that's all."

I left her on the sidewalk in front of the gym and walked back to my car. I told myself I didn't really feel her staring daggers into my back.

Just to make the lie I'd told inside the gym look good, I got in line at the gas station.

From where I sat waiting for the car in front of me to pull forward so I could get to a pump, I had a clear view of the front door of the gym.

Melody had gone back inside, but Mr. Muscles came out carrying a gym bag in one hand. With the other, he held a cell phone up to one ear. I watched him scan the parking lot as he walked over to the white SUV.

He stopped scanning when he saw my car.

How did he know what I drove? My car was a nondescript silver sedan which I'd scrimped to finish paying for after the divorce was final. The shape and color were the second most common in Reno after the ever popular SUV.

Melody might have told him, but I didn't think that was likely. In fact, I wasn't sure if she'd ever seen my car outside of the few times she'd been home when I'd dropped Samantha off for a weekend visit with Ryan.

I wasn't close enough to see the expression on Mr. Muscles' face.

I grabbed my camera from my purse and turned it on. Hell, if he was going to pose for me while he was staring at me, I might as well take advantage of the opportunity.

I balanced the camera on my steering wheel and zoomed in so that his face filled the display on the back of the camera. I snapped off a couple of shots before I realized that he was no longer talking on his cell phone. He had it held up in front of himself.

He was taking my picture with the phone, and he wasn't

being any more subtle about it than Justin Sewell had been standing in front of the cafe taking pictures of Melody as she headed for her car.

Only Mr. Muscles was doing something that Sewell hadn't done.

He was smiling.

## 9

I couldn't reach Kyle on his cell, and the desk clerk who answered the phone in the detective division told me that he wasn't available. Either he was still meeting with his witness or he'd gone out on a call. I'd have to give him the details about Mr. Muscles later.

I didn't want to call Ryan until I had information from Kyle, but given my little argument with Melody in front of the gym, I didn't want her to ambush him as soon as she could get him on the phone. Or, worse yet, pay an unannounced visit to his office and ambush him there.

I hadn't programmed Ryan's office number into my phone's auto dial. I'd told myself it was just one more snip of the ties that held us together. That was bull, of course. I knew the number by heart.

I waited until I finished pumping the little bit of gas I actually didn't need right then into my car. I drove out onto McCarran, found a McDonald's a few blocks away, and pulled into the drive thru for a large iced tea. While I waited, I called Ryan.

"I've got good news and bad news," I said. "Which do you want first?"

Ryan sighed. "It's been a bitch of a day. Give me the good news first."

"I've got two possible stalkers for you."

"Two?" Ryan asked.

"Possibly. I'll email you pictures when I get back to my office."

I gave him the information I had on Justin Sewell and the driver of the white SUV. I didn't tell him yet that the driver might be an undercover cop. I wouldn't pass that information along until I could confirm that fact with Kyle. For all I knew, Lewis Richards could have sold the SUV to someone else who hadn't reregistered it yet.

"You couldn't narrow it down?" he asked when I was done.

There it was, that slightly disappointed tone of voice I'd come to know so well during the last few years of our marriage.

"They were both doing stalkery things. It's not like I caught anyone hiding in a bush with a camera while wearing a raincoat and nothing underneath."

He was quiet for a beat. So was I.

"Sorry," he finally said. "It's been—"

"—a rough day." He hadn't apologized to me for a long time. It actually made me feel worse for what I had to tell him next. "You ready for the bad news?"

Another sigh. I could almost see him pinching the bridge of his nose.

"I ran into Melody at the gym," I said. "To say she wasn't happy to see me is an understatement."

"She saw you." He bit off each word like it left a bitter taste in his mouth.

"I didn't plan on it."

"Did you plan at all?"

Did I...

An angry retort popped into my head. Luckily for Ryan, the

people in the car ahead of me in the drive thru finally got their order, and it was my turn to pay for my iced tea.

Dealing with the cashier gave me a minute to cool off.

Ryan knew how to push my buttons. He'd learned well from my mother during our marriage. One of the favorite buttons he pushed, especially toward the end of our marriage, had to do with the one thing I'd tried to do as an investigator that I'd totally failed at: tracking down the hit-and-run driver who'd nearly killed Samantha.

When he really wanted to hurt me, he questioned my competence. That button only worked because deep down I questioned it, too.

But not this time around. It had only been bad timing that Melody had spotted me through that open door in the gym.

Wait a minute.

So what if Melody had spotted me? Reno's still a small town. People run into other people they know all the time. Why had she assumed I was at the gym because of her?

Ryan hadn't told her he'd hired me to find her stalker. As far as she knew, I was there investigating Mr. Muscles. Did she just assume that Ryan would ask me to follow her around, or that I would even agree to do something like that? She didn't know me well enough to figure out exactly how big of a sap I am. Most ex-wives would have told their ex-husbands to go take a flying leap.

Unless Mr. Muscles did have something to do with Melody. Something she cared about. Something she didn't want me to see.

Which brought me back around to the question of whether Mr. Muscles was still an undercover drug cop.

I'd apparently been quiet for too long. "Look, Abby," Ryan said. "I didn't mean..."

He did, but I let it drop.

"You need to know what happened," I said. I gave him a

quick, bullet-point summary of everything from the time I saw the SUV tail Melody from the cafe through the uncomfortable conversation in the gym. Everything except my phone call with Kyle, and the fact that Mr. Muscles had been snapping pictures of me.

"Okay," he said when I was done. "Send me what you've got."

I was already on the way back to my office, my iced tea safely ensconced in the cup holder and building up beads of sweat on the outside of the cardboard cup.

No wonder I was melting. Heat plus humidity, a rarity in my neck of the woods. Desert dwellers don't do humidity well.

"Give me about a half hour," I said. "I'll make a quick stop at the office, and then I can get back out on the street and pick up the surveillance after Melody leaves the gym."

"No. With any luck, what you've got will be enough to convince her to get a protective order against these guys. Especially—what did you call him?—Mr. Muscles? Go ahead and put together a bill for your time."

I blinked. He'd just fired me. Nicely, but he'd still fired me.

We'd gone from sharing our lives together to me invoicing him for services rendered.

Well, wasn't that just peachy. So much for being friends.

"Will do," I said. I ended the call before he could say anything else.

It took me five minutes of grumbling before I cooled down enough to realize that maybe this was the final wakeup call I'd needed. Ryan had Melody in his life now, for better or worse. He didn't need me anymore except in a professional capacity, and, as it turned out, he didn't even want me there.

Well, fine. He didn't have to tell me twice.

He could just go ahead and make a life with Melody and leave me out of it. If he had any more problems with Melody, he could leave me out of those as well.

I still had concerns about whether Melody's issues with an undercover drug cop might affect Samantha, but Ryan's next weekend with Samantha wasn't until Labor Day. By then I should know whether the guy driving the white SUV was Lewis Richards and if he was still working undercover.

In the meantime, I'd keep an eye out for my daughter like I always did, concentrate on my own life, and tell my inner sap to take a flying leap the next time she reared her ugly head.

Abby Maxon, woman of resolve.

## 10

T hat night I had a quick conversation on the phone with Kyle while I made a fancy dinner salad for Samantha and I to share while we watched the latest Robert Downey, Jr., movie on Blu-ray. To say he was relieved that I wasn't tailing the white SUV anymore was a vast under-statement.

Of course, I didn't tell him that Ryan had fired me. I may not have much in the pride department, but I do have a little.

"Richards still owns the SUV as far as I can tell," Kyle said. "Getting information on what he's working on is trickier. He's still on the force, but any information on his current assign-ment is strictly need to know, and I don't have an official need to know."

I gave Kyle the physical description of Mr. Muscles. Unfor-tunately, he couldn't tell me whether the guy had been Richards.

"When I busted him, he was a skinny little prick, but that's in line with an undercover stint as a druggie," Kyle said. "If he's beefed up now, he's either moved up in the ranks of the organization he was trying to infiltrate, or he's got a new assignment. I'd need a picture to be sure."

I'd downloaded all the pictures I'd taken of Mr. Muscles on my work computer and wiped them off my camera to free up space. I'd have to go to the office I shared downtown with a freelance writer. I didn't want to do that tonight.

For one thing, the writer worked nights and I worked days. The few times I'd shown up at night, I'd thought she was going to throw a box of cookies at me for interrupting her while she was writing.

Plus, I really wanted to chat with Samantha about the whole Jonathan visiting overnight thing. Which she still hadn't brought up on her own. Granted, it had only been one day, but my mommy radar was tingling. The kids had a plan up their sleeves, and I didn't like being the last one in the know.

"I can send you one tomorrow," I said to Kyle.

We chatted about a few other things, including where I might like to go on our Labor Day trip to San Francisco. Samantha would be staying with Ryan, and Kyle's daughter Lauren would be with her mother. Labor Day weekend was the first time our respective visitation schedules had worked out so that we both were child-free for an entire weekend. Labor Day would also be our first out of town trip together since we'd been dating.

I was excited about the trip, but I also felt odd about it. Up until today, it almost seemed like I was planning an illicit rendezvous that I shouldn't talk about to anyone, especially Ryan.

Now I didn't care what Ryan thought.

"You want to catch a ball game?" Kyle asked. He was a San Francisco Giants fan, and he'd mentioned before that the Giants would be in town that weekend.

I knew enough about baseball from when I'd been married to Ryan, a former high school jock who played every sport under the sun, to know that I wasn't that interested in baseball. I never went to a Reno Aces game, even though Norton Greenburger had offered me free tickets more than once, but a major league game might be different.

Besides, I'd be spending time with Kyle doing something that he enjoyed.

"You have tickets?" I asked, already knowing the answer.

"Well..." I could hear the smile in his voice. "I might have."

"Then we'd be silly not to go."

"I'll buy you a hat," he said.

"I don't wear hats." At least not baseball hats.

"You'd look cute in a hat."

Cute? "Are you trying to butter me up, officer?"

"Detective," he said. "I worked hard for that shield."

I had no doubt that he had. He worked hard at everything.

In the background, I could hear the squawk of a saxophone.

I winced. Kyle wasn't the only one in his family who worked hard for what they wanted.

"She's practicing again?" I asked.

He sighed. "I think I need to get a pair of those headphones you told me about."

We talked a few minutes more before we decided we better hang up, Kyle so he could convince his daughter to stop practicing long enough for a quick trip to the Best Buy store at Legends with a side trip to the frozen yogurt store for her, and me to finish the salad.

Samantha bustled into the kitchen when I was just about to pour dressing over the top.

"On the side!" she said, like I was drenching her food with poison.

I arched an eyebrow. "When did you get so high maintenance?"

She gave me The Look.

The one I was becoming increasingly more familiar with, and that I saw on her friend Maddie's face all the time.

The look that said moms are the dumbest, most out-of-step creatures on the face of the earth.

"Most of the calories in a salad are in the dressing," Samantha said. "Everybody knows that."

I did, in fact, know that. I just didn't care. I was a little concerned that Samantha did, although I supposed that sooner or later my now fashion-conscious daughter would also become my weight-conscious daughter.

Weight-conscious was one thing. Obsessive was another thing.

Samantha wasn't overweight in the least little bit. Maddie, who'd never been overweight either, was well on her way to becoming emaciated, as far as I was concerned. She'd lost more weight than she needed to over the summer, and I didn't like to think about how she'd done that. The last thing I wanted was for Samantha to follow in her friend's footsteps.

Not that I could say that. I'd learned from my relationship with my own mother that there was a fine line between comment and criticism from a kid's perspective.

"Okay," I said. "I'll put the dressing down and slowly back away from the salad."

I did just that, and I got the hoped-for response: Samantha giggled.

"You're just lucky I didn't decide to serve cheeseburgers and chili-cheese fries," I said.

"Yuck." Samantha plucked a small slice of lunch meat from the salad. Smoked turkey, thinly sliced. "You know that stuff's not good for you."

This from the girl who'd shared a banana split with Jonathan a mere eight months ago.

Samantha carried the salad into the living room and put it on the coffee table. I followed with a tall glass of iced tea for me and plain water for her. While I sat down on the couch, she popped in the movie.

We ate our dressing-free salads in companionable silence while Robert Downey, Jr., and a bunch of other extremely fit and good-looking men, women, and demi-gods went about saving the planet.

Samantha thought Robert Downey, Jr., was pretty good looking "for an older guy," but I had dibs on the demi-god with the blond hair and big hammer, a weapon whose name I couldn't pronounce if I tried.

When the movie was over, Samantha took charge of the remote and searched through the Blu-ray's special features.

Now or never, I thought to myself. Might as well plunge right in.

"So," I said. "Jonathan's mother tells me you're thinking of inviting him to spend a night or two here instead of just a day visit."

Samantha froze for only a split second before she kept on scanning through the special features menu. "It seems silly to waste that much gas on such a short visit," she said. "We were thinking that maybe over Labor Day weekend he could come here for a day or two."

Labor Day. Jonathan would be having a long weekend that weekend, too.

"You're supposed to be with your dad that weekend," I said. "Have you run this by him?"

Samantha didn't say anything.

"He might have other plans for you," I said.

He might also have something to say about housing a boy he hadn't even met yet. Or heard about, except from me.

Samantha looked down at the remote in her hand. "I was hoping I didn't have to go. I'd rather stay here."

She knew that I had plans to go to San Francisco with Kyle.

While I might have felt weird about mentioning the trip to

Ryan, I'd kept my relationship with Kyle out in the open as far as my daughter was concerned. To a point. I wasn't about to discuss my sex life with my teenaged daughter, but I figured she knew that part already, even if she didn't want to think about it.

"I'm not going to be home that weekend," I said.

She shot me a quick sideways glance. "I could always stay with Maddie. I'm sure her mom wouldn't mind if Jonathan—"

"Not gonna happen," I said.

"Mom!" She drew the word out like she used to when she was in her terrible toddler stage and we had frequent battles of will. "You don't like any of my friends."

So much for having a logical conversation about this subject.

"You know that's not true," I said. "We've talked about Maddie. I like Maddie. I still like Maddie. That doesn't mean I'm not worried she's involved in things I don't want you involved in."

"So you don't trust me to think for myself when I'm around her."

I gestured at the salad plates littered with the remains of dressing-free lettuce and bits of lunch meat. "You never worried about the calories in a tablespoon of dressing before this summer when Maddie lost all that weight. Or about fitting into designer jeans before she started wearing them."

Samantha turned away from me to glare at the television where the heroes of the movie were frozen on the screen.

"Look, we can talk about Jonathan spending more than a couple of hours here," I said. "Just not over Labor Day weekend. His mother seems open to the idea. I'm not opposed to it."

"Fine."

It wasn't, not with her, not the way she said it, but I'd take it as a start.

She carried the empty salad plates to the kitchen, declined

my offer of popcorn for dessert, and said she was going to the den to work on a new piece.

Loud piano music began to fill the house almost imme-diately.

At least her anger seemed genuine, and she hadn't put on an act about Labor Day just to get me to capitulate to the idea of Jonathan staying overnight at some point. Up until this summer, I wouldn't have considered the possibility where Samantha was concerned, but it looked like my daughter was finally hitting the point in her life where she'd begin pulling away from me. I knew it had to happen one day, but I still wasn't ready for it.

I definitely wasn't ready for the men who knocked on my door a half hour later.

# 11

I 'm not exactly anti-social, but other than Kyle or one of Samantha's friends, the only person who ever rings my doorbell after eight o'clock at night, even in the summer when the sun's still up, is my neighbor Freddie March.

After Ryan and I split up, Freddie took it upon himself to be my little helper, whether I needed it or not. He and his wife Bess had lived in the neighborhood long before Ryan and I bought the house I still lived in.

Freddie had made enough money in the early days of the tech industry to retire comfortably far sooner than I ever would. He worked in his yard and watched sports on television and was the first person in the neighborhood to put up holiday decorations.

He was also a letch, but I cut him a little more slack these days since he'd helped me out last December. Freddie had called 9-1-1 when I really needed the cops but the killers who'd kidnapped me wouldn't let me make the call myself.

If I sound a little flip about what happened, I'm not.

I'm very aware of the fact that I could have been killed in my own house. Stuff like that makes a person appreciate the little things, like the fact that your letch of a neighbor actually has a good heart.

I still didn't accept Freddie's offers to mow the lawn for me or take out the trash—those offers would have had strings attached, I was sure, and besides, I liked Bess—but I no longer pretended I wasn't home whenever he brought over some of Bess's homemade cookies or a flyer for a neighborhood garage sale that I had no desire to participate in.

When the doorbell rang fifteen minutes into Samantha's latest loud classical music piano-fest, I expected to find Freddie on my doorstep asking me if I could get my daughter to tone it down just a bit because he was trying to watch the game.

Instead, when I looked through the narrow little window on one side of the door, I saw two men in rumpled suits.

No one wears suits in the middle of a Nevada summer to pay a visit to a stranger's house unless they're on official business. The fact that their suits were rumpled ruled out that these guys were lawyers or federal agents.

The fact that there were two of them told me it was serious.

After the mess at my house last December, I'd had a metal security door installed in front of my front door. To the casual observer it looked like a heavy-duty screen door, but the door had a deadbolt lock fitted into a metal doorframe attached to my house by some serious-looking hardware. Not impregnable by any means, but it made me feel better.

I always kept the security door locked whenever I was home. It definitely made me feel better now as I opened my front door to these two strange men.

"Abby Maxon?" the shorter of the two asked. He had about ten years on me, but where he stood on my front stoop, he was shorter than I was. The house was one step up from the stoop, so I figured he was maybe my height or just a little taller. His dark hair was shot through with gray, and his neck strained against his shirt and tie.

Instead of answering, I lifted an eyebrow. "Do I know you?" I asked.

"Are you Abby Maxon?" the other guy asked. He was younger and taller and blond, and I could see the hint of a five o'clock shadow glinting in the last of the summer sunlight.

This time I didn't say anything at all.

The two cops—and by now I'd figured out that they were cops; between the suits and their attempt at intimidation, they couldn't be anything else—shared a quick glance.

The shorter, older cop was closer to the door. He took his ID out of a pocket and held it up for me to look at.

According to his ID, he was Detective Vincent Archulette of the Reno Police Department.

Detective?

"And you?" I asked the younger cop.

His expression still neutral, he held up his ID. Detective Martin Squires. Also Reno Police Department.

I breathed a mental sigh of relief.

They weren't from the Sparks Police Department, which meant they weren't here because something had happened to Kyle.

Enough of the officers Kyle worked with knew the two of us were dating that if anything horrible happened to him, they'd let me know. The very worst notifications were always done in person, never over the phone.

Which meant these two were at my front door about something else.

I'd talked to a lot of police officers either through the investigations I did for Norton Greenburger or the accident investigation work I did for other attorneys. I'd never met these two before, and I wasn't sure I liked the official tone of their visit.

"What can I do for you, detectives?" I asked when they put their IDs away.

Detective Archulette sighed. "You're Abby Maxon, right?"

Norton always pounded into his clients that they shouldn't admit anything to police officers who showed up unannounced, but Norton wasn't dating a police officer. I had a slightly different perspective. Archulette had won me over a bit with that sigh. It told me he'd had a long day, just like I had.

"That's me," I said. "Can I help you with something?"

"Can we come inside?" Archulette asked.

A particularly loud and discordant noise came from the den where Samantha was still pounding away on the piano. Archulette winced.

"My daughter's working off some steam," I said. "It's probably quieter around back."

I unlocked the door and let the detectives inside. I offered them iced tea. They both declined, and we walked through the house and into the backyard.

Neither Ryan nor I were big into gardening, but he'd felt it important to put in the type of landscaping appropriate to a successful lawyer.

The backyard had a fire pit, a covered patio that was bigger than my living room, a built-in barbecue, and a water feature that included a fountain and a pond that used to have koi fish the size of small trout. Ryan took the fish when we split up and I told him that if he left the fish for me to feed, I'd feed them to the cat.

I wouldn't have, not really, but the fish had never been my favorite part of the backyard. I'm not sure what he did with them since he doesn't have a pond big enough for them at the condo. He never said and I never asked.

Ryan took the upscale patio furniture we used to have, which was fine with me. I had a small glider swing and some inexpensive lawn chairs I'd picked up at a garage sale, and that was enough for me. My days of catered patio parties were long gone, and good riddance.

The sun had ducked down behind the hills to the west, and

the worst of the day's heat was leaching into the night sky. An evening breeze rustled the leaves in the oak tree along my back fence, and the neighbor's kids on the other side of Freddie March's house were splashing around in their pool.

A typical summer evening in suburbia, and here I was, entertaining two detectives.

I sat on the glider.

Archulette sat down on one of the lawn chairs. Squires stayed on his feet, feigning interest in the fire pit.

"How old's your daughter?" Archulette asked.

"Sixteen," I said.

"Fun age."

I recognized the small talk for an attempt to put me at ease. I decided to go with it and see where it went.

"You have kids?" I asked.

"Two girls," Archulette said. "One thirteen, one just starting college. Squires there, he's smart. He's still single. No kids."

Squires gave him a nod and a fleeting smile that had no humor to it. Squires would never be the good cop. I had the feeling Archulette had more practice at it.

"You married?" Archulette asked.

Something twitched along the back of my neck at the question, almost like my subconscious had picked up on some subtle change of tone or posture that I hadn't otherwise noticed.

"Divorced," I said, although I had a feeling Archulette already knew the answer.

Archulette nodded. "You know a woman named Melody Hartwell?"

Squires had stopped looking at the fire pit. He was studying me instead.

Whatever this visit was about, it had something to do with Melody. The sudden chill in my fingertips had nothing to do with the evening breeze.

"My ex-husband's fiancé," I heard myself say.

It was Squires who asked the next question. "Can you account for your whereabouts between four and six this afternoon?"

They were asking if I had an alibi. Cops don't ask about alibis unless they're investigating something serious.

I'd been home with Samantha from a little after four. I hadn't left, and I was pretty sure Freddie March could verify that, but I wasn't about to tell these two cops any of that.

Not yet, and not without Norton in the room with me.

"Well?" Squires asked.

"I think I'm done answering questions," I said.

"We can take you downtown," Squires said.

I nodded, hoping that my face didn't betray how fast my heart was beating.

"That you can," I said. "And I can have my lawyer meet us there."

The two cops shared a look. Archulette sighed again.

"That's only going to work once," I said.

Archulette actually looked a little guilty. "Had to try," he said.

Right. "Look," I said. "I like cops. I'm dating a cop. I want to help you guys out, but if I'm a suspect, it's not in my best interests to talk without my lawyer present."

"Who's your lawyer?" Archulette asked.

I gave him Norton's name. "I work for him, part-time. He'd probably fire me if he knew I'd agreed to talk to you at all without him."

Archulette held my gaze for a minute.

After all the years I'd been married to Ryan, not to mention all the years I'd been an investigator, I was pretty good at waiting people out. Most people tried to fill uncomfortable silences by rambling on, usually about themselves. It was something investigators counted on. I know I did. Kyle told me once that cops did, too, and that I was one of the best he'd ever seen at waiting people out.

Easy to do when I was the one looking for information. I was discovering fast that out-waiting a cop was more difficult when the cop in question was treating me like a suspect, but I did my best not to fidget.

"Okay," Archulette said. "Here's the thing."

He leaned forward in the lawn chair, elbows resting on his knees, hands clasped loosely in front of him. Squires stood behind Archulette, arms crossed over his chest, his face expressionless.

"Somebody torched Melody Hartwell's car this afternoon," Archulette said. He looked hard at me, and I realized that he could do the bad cop stare as well as his partner. "Ass end of an empty lot downtown. Nobody saw anything. A passing motorist called it in."

He stopped talking, but it was just a pause for effect. There was something else coming. Something bad. I wasn't sure I wanted to hear it. Archulette didn't give me a choice.

"The thing is," he said, "Melody Hartwell was in her car at the time."

# 12

Two hours later, I was in an interview room at the Reno Police Department with Norton Greenburger.

Detectives Archulette and Squires sat on the other side of a plain metal table that had been bolted to the floor. The straight-back chairs weren't bolted to the floor and I wasn't in handcuffs. I wasn't technically under arrest, but the detectives had made it clear to Norton that I was a "person of interest."

I'd had a hurried conversation with Norton in a private room little bigger than a closet that Norton assured me had no hidden recording devices. I'd expected him to read me the riot act for talking to the detectives at my house. Instead he'd asked for a bullet-point outline of my day.

I told him everything that had happened, right down to Mr. Muscles taking my picture with his cell phone and Ryan firing me for letting myself be seen by Melody.

"Ryan can clear this up," I'd said to Norton, then it really hit me—Ryan's fiancé was dead.

Why the hell hadn't he called to let me know?

Was he really that pissed at me that he felt he couldn't lean on me for support?

So pissed off that he'd let Detectives Frick and Frack blindside me?

I made myself take a deep breath. Ryan probably wasn't in any shape to talk to anyone about anything.

I felt like a shit for my internal rant, brief as it was. His world had just fallen apart. I had no reason to expect that the first person he'd call would be me.

"You don't need Ryan," Norton had said. "Not right now. What you're going to concentrate on right now it sticking to the simple facts of your day. You're an investigator. You were hired to investigate. That's all you did. It's possible you saw something these officers can use in their investigation. If I jump in and interrupt the questioning, you stop talking. Are we clear on that?"

I'd nodded. Easy concept to grasp. Much harder to apply.

The official recorded interview with the detectives started out easy. They asked specific questions, and I gave them specific answers. When did Ryan call me, what did he want me to do, where had I gone that day, what had I seen Melody do. Those questions were easy to answer. All I had to do was repeat the bullet points I'd already gone over with Norton.

When they asked what made Ryan think Melody had a stalker, Norton interrupted. "My client can't answer as to Mr. Maxon's state of mind," he said. "You'll have to ask him."

"Good enough," Archulette said. "But something must have made him think this guy your client was supposed to uncover was dangerous."

I started to say something, but Norton's hand on my knee stopped me.

"Again," Norton said. "That's a question you'll have to direct to Mr. Maxon."

Archulette grunted. "Do you often take dangerous assignments?" he asked me.

I waited to see if Norton was going to say something, but he didn't.

Archulette's question made me think of the conversation I'd had with Jonathan's mother. I didn't think any of the assignments I took were dangerous, although at least one had turned out that way.

"That's hard to answer," I said. "I suppose it depends on what you think is dangerous."

"Dangerous to you," Archulette said.

"No," I said.

"Why?" This question came from Squires, who so far had let Archulette take the lead.

I glanced at Squires. "I think your partner knows the answer to that question."

"Your kid," Archulette said.

I nodded.

"Was that a 'yes'?" Squires asked.

I took a breath instead of making a smart-ass remark.

My kid was currently cooling her heels at Bess and Freddie March's house. I'd told her briefly what had happened to Melody. She hadn't cried, but she'd said she felt bad for her dad and sorry that anyone had to die like that. She'd been subdued when I walked her over to the Marches under the watchful eye of the detectives.

Tonight was definitely one night I'd rather be with my daughter helping her process her feelings about the sudden, violent death of a woman she hadn't liked rather than spending the night being grilled by Detectives Frick and Frack.

And that's just what this was.

Sure, Archulette's questions were mild so far. He was letting Squires come in with the zingers. But I had no doubt they'd be just as happy to pin what happened to Melody on me if they thought they could make the charges stick.

I made my expression as neutral as I could under the circumstances. "Yes," I said. "I'm a single mother. The choices I make in my work affect my daughter, so I don't deliberately take dangerous assignments."

Norton didn't wince when I said "deliberately," but even I knew I shouldn't have said that. It gave Archulette an opening, and he took it.

"Deliberately." Archulette leaned forward just a little. "What about by accident? Like when you're doing a favor for your ex?"

"Ryan hired me," I said.

"Hired you," Archulette said. "He works for a big firm, right? Doesn't the firm have their own investigators?"

"My client wouldn't know that," Norton said. "You'd have to ask—"

"—Mr. Maxon," Archulette said. "Don't worry. I will. So your ex wants to hire you. Why did you agree to the job? It couldn't have been fun, trailing around after the new woman in your ex's life."

I'd asked myself that more than once that day, especially after I ran into Melody at the gym. I could have said it was for the money, which would have been partly true. But the real reason was simple.

"He asked," I said.

"So you do anything he asks?" Squires said.

"We have an amicable relationship," I said. "I try to be amenable when I can."

"Even though he dumped you for a new woman," Squires said. "I find that hard to believe."

Norton sighed. "Gentlemen, it's getting late. Too late for a fishing expedition when you don't even know if there are fish in the lake. Let me make this simple for you."

His voice was calm and cool, but there was steel in his eyes.

Norton Greenburger wasn't a big man, but he could be impressive when he wanted to be. He was at least sixty, still worked out obsessively, and had a reputation as one of the best criminal defense attorneys in Reno, if not in the state. Even though I knew Norton got to the office every morning shortly after seven, he was still going strong after eleven at night.

"When you attempted to get a statement from my client at her home, outside the presence of her counsel," Norton said, emphasizing the last few words, "you asked if she could account for her whereabouts between four and six this afternoon. The short answer is yes, she can, and we'll be happy to file an alibi if it comes to that. My client is not your suspect, nor is she a person of interest. She was hired to conduct an investigation, which she did. Since the job she'd been hired for was complete, she sent a final report and bill to her client." He stood up, sliding the chair noisily across the linoleum floor. "That, as they say, is that." He paused for a moment, staring in turns at Archulette, then Squires, and then back to Archulette. "Either book her, or we're leaving."

At the words "book her," my heart started beating double time. I did not want to spend the night in jail. I didn't deserve to spend the night in jail. I knew it, Norton knew it, didn't the detectives know it, too?

Archulette smiled, but it had no humor to it.

I tried not to think ill of the man. He was just doing his job, and he was clearly as tired as the rest of us, but he was also a chess player.

Detectives had to be always thinking three or more moves ahead. Kyle told me that the first detective he had as a partner had insisted that Kyle learn how to play chess. Kyle was trying to teach me now, but I wasn't the best student.

Archulette had brought me in to see if I would slip up and say something they could use. They clearly wanted information about Ryan, which worried me. They couldn't actually think Ryan had anything to do with Melody's death, could they? Ryan loved her. He'd only wanted to protect her from the kind of crazy people we both knew were out there. He must be devastated by her murder.

"You and your client are free to go, Mr. Greenburger," Squires said, then he turned his cold gaze on me. "We're going to want a look at the contents of that report you sent your ex. Are we going to need a search warrant?"

"That depends on whether Mr. Maxon authorizes my client to release the report," Norton said. "We are more than willing to cooperate with your investigation provided your inquiries don't delve into areas involving client confidentiality. In that case, we'll either need to get authorization from Mr. Maxon or you'll have to get a warrant."

I had no desire to see my office torn apart by the police department in a search for whatever information I'd uncovered about Melody.

Or my home, for that matter.

I tried not to bring my work home, but sometimes it was unavoidable. I hadn't done any work on this case at home. That didn't mean the cops wouldn't include my house in the warrant.

I would gladly give the detectives whatever information I could to keep that from happening, but Norton hadn't had time to go over the quick report I'd sent to Ryan. He'd be looking at everything I'd done from a lawyer's perspective, keeping the worst case scenario firmly in mind.

What was the worst case here? I'd end up in jail.

I hadn't done anything wrong, but I wasn't naive enough to think that would keep me in the clear.

Somewhere along the line, someone had mentioned my involvement with Melody, and that had been enough to put the cops on my case. Plus, if the cops had talked to any of the people who'd seen me with Melody at the gym, they'd know that our little scene, while not exactly a knock-down, drag-out battle, had been tense.

Circumstantial evidence was still evidence, and people had been arrested for less.

The next worst case scenario was that the cops would arrest Ryan. I didn't think for one minute that he was capable of killing anyone, much less Melody. The man I'd married was highly competitive—most trial lawyers were—but competitive didn't mean homicidal.

The detectives were on the wrong track, they just couldn't see that yet. In their world, murders often started with domestic disputes, and the spouse or significant other was always a person of interest until they were proven not to be.

I hoped to hell that Ryan had an airtight alibi. His nice, ordered life had already been blown to hell. Being the subject of a homicide investigation was only going to make it worse. And while the cops were concentrating the murder investigation on the wrong guy, the person who actually killed Melody would still be out walking around. He might even be looking for the next person to kill.

Now wasn't that a cheery thought.

## 13

B efore he let me leave to go home, Norton said he wanted to have a little chat with me. That was fine. I was still keyed up and too many things were bouncing around in my brain to let me unwind.

"I want you to send me that report you sent to Ryan," Norton said as soon as we were outside the police station. "I'll look it over first thing in the morning. In fact, send me everything you have on the case, all the photographs you took, all the notes you made. If there's nothing in the report that could bite you in the ass, I'll contact Ryan and get his authorization to send it to the police."

"What about the rest of it? I didn't put everything in report." I told Norton about the possibility that Mr. Muscles at the gym was an undercover cop named Lewis Richards who was the registered owner of the white SUV that had followed Melody from the cafe on California to the gym. "I didn't want to give Ryan that information until I could confirm it with Kyle."

"I'll keep that in mind. If Kyle finds out, let me know, but don't do anything on your own to find out." Norton gave me a level—if tired—no nonsense stare. "You're hands off on this one from now on, Abby, no joke. You don't want to be seen as interfering with a police investigation, especially not one where you and your ex are under suspicion."

The police department in Sparks where Kyle had his office was still on the edge of the city, close enough to housing developments to be a part of Sparks proper but still near enough the foothills to the east of the city to feel open and somewhat set apart.

The building housing the Reno Police Department was smack in downtown Reno, taking up a roughly triangular lot bordered by High Street, Second Street, and Kuenzli. The Truckee River curved along the back side of what used to be a public parking lot at the rear of the building, but what now housed only police vehicles.

That was fine with me. I hadn't wanted to park anywhere near the station anyway. I'd found a space on Kuenzli where it didn't feel like I was giving up any of my independence. Probably not a logical response, but I didn't think I'd been reacting from pure logic ever since the detectives had told me Melody had been murdered.

As Norton and I talked, we walked down the sidewalk toward my car.

We were only about a block or so away from the new Reno Aces ballpark. There'd been no home game tonight, so the neighborhood was relatively quiet and deserted. At least as quiet and deserted as downtown Reno gets near midnight on a midweek summer night.

No clouds blotted out the night sky, and the heat of the day was finally gone. I couldn't see many stars overhead—the neon lights on the casinos in the downtown core kept all but the brightest stars in shadow—but I could smell the faint odor of the river and a late-blooming flower garden on the other side of the street.

All in all, it might have been a pleasant walk except for the reason I was downtown so late.

Now that the interview was over, I couldn't stop shaking inside. I'd never been a suspect in any crime, much less a murder, and a murder of someone I knew at that. Melody had been a vibrant, beautiful woman. I might have hated her from time to time—what wife wouldn't hate the woman her husband had left her for?—but that didn't mean I couldn't feel sorrow over her death.

Sorrow, and an overwhelming need to protect my family. Samantha, most definitely, but also Ryan. He would always be the father of my child, and that meant he would always be family, no matter what our personal issues were. Norton was smart enough to know that.

"I can't promise you that I'll just sit on my hands on this," I said. "I won't interfere, but I won't let the police railroad Ryan either."

He nodded, and then looked over his shoulder. From where we stood, we could see the top of the baseball stadium over the trees that lined the river.

"I never thought Reno could sustain a minor league team, not after the Silversox," he said.

I vaguely remembered the old ballpark out on Moana Lane where the Silversox used to play. With its wooden outfield fences and battered bleachers, it had looked like every rundown minor league ballpark in every local-kid-gets-a-shot-at-the-majors baseball movie ever made.

The old Silversox ballpark was gone now, bulldozed away in the name of progress. My dad had gone to a few games there, but baseball hadn't been a passion with him, especially not minor league ball, and his interest in the Sox had eventually faded. I couldn't even remember when the team finally stopped playing here.

The Aces, on the other hand, seemed to be doing great if

the traffic jams in the area every time they had a home game were anything to go by.

"Sometimes things surprise me," Norton said. "Somebody comes along with a good idea and they work hard to see that idea come to life. Pour everything they have into it. They overcome setbacks, re-evaluate priorities, regroup and charge again if necessary. Won't let anything stop them even if conventional wisdom says they're nuts. And sometimes, just sometimes, it all works out in the end."

Something changed in his expression, almost like the fire that had sustained him was in danger of going out, and for the first time since I'd known him, I thought he actually looked his age.

Give him a few more years, and he'd probably be sending a younger associate to these late-night interrogations.

"I hope you surprise me," he said. "I've seen too many people go off in the wrong direction, all full of piss and vinegar, as my mother used to say. So fired up they can't see beyond their own convictions, and they don't realize they're setting themselves up for a fall. Don't do that, Abby."

I started to say something in my own defense, but he held a hand up to stop me.

"You're a good investigator or I wouldn't have hired you, not even part time, but right now you're driven by your emotions. This whole thing is too personal. You can't separate your head from your heart. I saw it in there, and I can see it now."

I couldn't argue that point. He was right.

"There's a reason for that saying—I know you've heard it—that a lawyer who represents himself has a fool for a client," he said. "Don't be a fool. Lawyers aren't god, no matter what we'd like to believe. I can only do so much to protect you."

The streetlights blurred as my emotions kicked in with a vengeance. The last thing I wanted to do was cry in front of Norton, and I blinked to make sure I wouldn't.

"I'll be fine." My voice was thick and unsteady, but if Norton noticed, he didn't say anything. He just patted my shoulder once, then he turned around and walked back toward the other side of the police station where he must have left his own car.

Instead of getting in my car, I crossed Kuenzli and walked down the deserted sidewalk until I was standing on the bridge.

The water in the river looked nearly black at this time of night. The Truckee wasn't a big river as rivers go, but the water was icy cold even during the dog days of summer. Deceptively lazy, the river was deep enough and the water flowed fast enough that people had drowned in the Truckee because they didn't respect it.

I was all too aware of how that lesson applied to the situation I found myself in.

I respected the power of the police department and the power of the courts. I'd spent too many years on the periphery of the legal system not to respect it. I also knew, deep in my gut, that the police weren't going to leave me or Ryan alone until they had another viable suspect.

A body found in a burning car was going to make the local news. The involvement of a long-time local attorney might make it headline material. The cops were going to want to wrap this case as quickly as possible, and if that meant building a case on circumstantial evidence, so be it.

Ryan was going to need my help. But there was one more reason I couldn't drop this even though Norton wanted me to.

As I stood there watching the river flow beneath me, I finally let myself shed tears for the woman who'd replaced me in Ryan's life. The woman who'd been trying to build a relationship with my daughter for my ex-husband's sake.

I couldn't drop this case because of Melody.

Whether I hated her or not, she deserved better than to die the way she had. Hell, she'd deserved better than the way I'd treated her on occasion.

I hadn't known her well in life, but the one thing I could do for her in death was make sure the right person went to prison for her murder.

# 14

Norton called me at seven-thirty the next morning.

I was still asleep when my cell phone *dong-donged* at me. Samantha had programmed the iconic two notes from *Law & Order* on my cell for Norton's ringtone. She'd said it was either that or the two notes from *Jaws*. Either one would have fit, but neither ringtone was particularly demanding. I'd been up until after three, the hamster on the wheel in my head refusing to stop chasing my discordant thoughts around my brain, and it took me a minute to realize Norton was trying to reach me.

Had he heard something about Ryan? I'd tried to call Ryan on the way to the police station last night, but the call had gone straight through to voicemail. There'd been no messages on my phone after I'd left the police station, and none on my answering machine at home.

I struggled awake and managed to croak out something that might have been hello.

There was a slight pause. "Abby? Did I wake you?"

Norton sounded as awake as he always did. Of course, trial

lawyers, whether civil or criminal, lived with constant stress. They either coped or went insane. Norton had probably learned long ago how to turn off his thoughts enough to go to sleep at a semi-reasonable hour.

"'s okay." I rubbed my hand over my face, trying to rub the remnants of sleep away. "Have you heard from Ryan? I couldn't reach him last night."

"He's being represented by Patrick Rosen. I talked to Pat before I called you. He said Ryan's a mess."

Patrick Rosen was one of Ryan's partners in their law practice. He was also a top flight criminal defense attorney, almost as good as Norton. I went cold inside at the thought that Ryan needed that kind of representation.

"So he's a suspect?" I asked.

"Not officially. So far the police aren't naming any suspects. They questioned him like they questioned you, although I imagine Pat didn't let Ryan talk as much as I let you talk."

I knew that was smart from a legal standpoint. I'd been in shock, but I'd still been able to think. Ryan was a good lawyer, but even the best lawyer can't think like a lawyer when their world has been shattered. Ryan had always been good about keeping his cool, but I'd seen him come unglued at the hospital when Samantha nearly died.

"Pat thinks, as do I, that you and Ryan should keep contact between you to a minimum, at least until the police focus the investigation elsewhere," Norton said. "Pat said Ryan seemed to agree with that. Anything vital, you can handle it through me."

Okay. So I couldn't talk to Ryan. My instinct was to rebel against that. It was an old hot button issue I'd had with my mother—*you can't tell me what to do, I'm a grown woman!*—that I apparently hadn't outgrown. But if Ryan agreed and the lawyers thought it best, I'd take their advice.

"What about Samantha?" I asked. "What if she wants to talk to her dad, or see him?"

Samantha had been a sad, sleepy girl when I'd picked her up from the Marches the night before. I'd apologized profusely to the Marches for being so late. Bess had only given me a hug. Freddie, in a rare show of restraint, had stood behind his wife, hands in his pockets, and told me how sorry he was about the whole sorry thing.

Once we got back home, Samantha had wanted to cuddle like she hadn't for months. So I'd sat with her on her bed, arm around her shoulders, while she talked about not knowing what to do or say to her dad but feeling like she should mend the rift that had grown between them. I hadn't known how to respond to that—nothing I could have said would have made anything better—so I'd just held her until she finally started to drift off to sleep.

"Of course, Samantha can see her dad." Norton knew that Ryan and I had joint custody, even though Samantha spent most of her time with me. "When's the next planned visitation?"

"Labor Day weekend."

I didn't mention that Samantha might have other plans. All of our lives had changed drastically overnight. All of our plans, including my trip to San Francisco with Kyle, might be on hold indefinitely.

And I still hadn't heard from Kyle. I'd called him on my way to the police station as well. My call had gone straight to voicemail.

"What about phone calls?" I asked. Norton hesitated, and a chill worked its way down my spine. "What aren't you telling me?"

"Ryan's going to be under a microscope. Samantha can call him if she wants, but he's in trouble, and he knows it. He might not be in the best frame of mind to talk to his daughter."

"I thought you said he's not a suspect."

"I said he wasn't an 'official' suspect, but he's the primary person of interest. Circumstantial evidence points to him, and I know how the cops will view it."

"What circumstantial evidence?" I asked.

Norton didn't respond.

"You know I'm going to find out," I said. "You might as well tell me now and save us both the aggravation."

"All right. Ryan admitted to getting into an argument with Melody at his office. He met with her behind closed doors, but they got loud, staff in his office heard, and Melody stormed out. That part's in the official statement he gave the police."

"There's more, isn't there?"

"I imagine there is, and I imagine Ryan's told Pat, but I'm not privileged to that information and neither are you. Abby, I looked at the report you prepared for Ryan as well as the photographs. You admit that you were following Melody the entire day at his request, and that you had a confrontation with her a short time before she died. I'm not sure you understand what a truly precarious situation you're in. If the police can make a case against Ryan, you could be charged as an accessory."

"What?" If I'd thought I'd been in shock last night, it was nothing compared to this. "How could they possibly..."

Of course, they could. The case would be purely circum-stantial, but a good prosecutor could make me look like Lizzie Borden without the axe.

"Do you understand now?" Norton said. "Why you and Ryan can't be seen together, talking about anything together, without it looking to the police like you're covering for each other?"

"God, Norton." My hand was trembling holding the cell phone. "She had a damn stalker. She might have had two of them. Stalkers are seriously whacked out people. You know that. I know that. Why aren't the cops focusing on them?"

"They will. That's why I've got Ryan's permission to show them the report, and I'd like yours regarding the rest of the information you didn't put in the report, including all the other photographs you sent me."

I'd interrupted the writer the night before when I'd stopped at my office to email Norton a copy of everything I had regarding my surveillance of Melody Hartwell. The writer had been too surprised at my sudden appearance to gripe at me for ruining the flow of her work or lob anything in my direction. Not that she'd been typing when I unlocked the office door. I didn't understand writers, but then again, I'm not sure she understood my work either.

"They'd be able to get all that with a warrant, right?" I asked.

"They can certainly make an argument for probable cause, so yes, I believe they'd get everything connected with your investigation one way or the other."

I sighed. I didn't like the idea of the cops digging through my files, but if it kept them from tearing apart my office and my house, I could live with it.

"Go ahead," I said. "You've got my permission to release all of it."

"Good," Norton said.

He hung up after telling me to take care of myself and that if he saw me at his office today attempting any other work, he'd fire me.

I sat in my bed, my arms wrapped around my knees, and stared at the thumb drive I'd left on my nightstand. I'd made it the night before at my office after I'd emailed copies of everything I had on Melody's case to Norton. It held a duplicate of everything on my office computer about Melody's stalkers.

As soon as I got myself together, I intended to go through everything on that thumb drive with a fine-tooth comb. The police would be going over all my files, but they'd be looking at the pictures and notes for evidence they could use against Ryan. I had a different purpose in mind. I intended to use my files as a starting point to prove Ryan was innocent.

# 15

Samantha was still asleep when I plugged the thumb drive into my laptop.

I'd brought the laptop out to my dining room table so I wouldn't disturb her. She usually slept with her door only partly closed in case the cat wanted to curl up on her bed. This morning the cat was grooming on the living room couch, stretched out in a pool of sunlight streaming in through the front window.

The day had all the promise of being a scorcher. I didn't know why a cat, who came equipped with a permanent fur coat, would seek out a sunny spot on a hot day, but this wasn't the first time I'd seen her do it.

Since I wasn't going to Norton's office and had no plans to go to my own, I'd slipped on a light cotton blouse and a pair of shorts. Instead of coffee, I was already drinking iced tea. The cat could keep the nice sunny spot all to herself. The dining room was still nice and cool.

My laptop was a few years out of date, and it didn't have the biggest screen. I planned to replace it someday, although as long as it kept working, someday kept being pushed further and further into the future. Right now it was good enough for what I needed.

Except for the rather terse written report I'd created in a hurry for Ryan, most of the digital files I had regarding my surveillance of Melody were the pictures I'd taken on my camera. I had a digital voice recorder that I used as well, but the only things I'd recorded were the addresses of the places Melody had gone and the times she arrived and departed so I could be precise in my written report.

The digital recorder was still in my purse, and I hadn't downloaded the recordings to my computer. I'd have to remember to ask Norton if he wanted copies of my voice files to give to the cops along with the rest of it.

When I'd looked at all my files last night, I'd been surprised to discover that I'd taken over a hundred pictures. The vast majority were of the two guys I'd spotted outside the cafe. Or more precisely, of Justin Sewell and the white SUV Lewis Richards owned.

As I scrolled through the photographs, one shot made me catch my breath. I'd been focused on Justin Sewell, trying to get a good picture of him to show to Ryan, but I'd caught Melody in the photo as well. She'd been walking to her car. What I hadn't seen when I was actually at the cafe taking the shot came through clear in the picture: Melody had turned around to glance at Justin, and she was smiling.

It didn't look like a simple smile, either.

I zoomed in until her face filled the frame. Unlike all those TV shows where the computer automatically filled in a blurry shot, the more I zoomed in on Melody's face, the fuzzier the picture got. So I pushed the computer toward the other side of the table and scooted back in my chair until I had enough distance that the picture looked more like a photograph again instead of a random collection of colorful pixels.

The photograph had caught Melody doing something she

probably hadn't wanted anyone to see, especially not anyone connected with Ryan. She'd been flirting with Justin Sewell. She might not have given him a little finger wave or a raised eyebrow, come hither look, but there was more to her smile than what a woman would give a strange man on the street who couldn't take his eyes off her.

Yesterday when I'd watched her leave the cafe by herself, I'd wondered who she'd had lunch with. Sure, it was possible she'd spent forty-five minutes inside having lunch by herself. I ate lunch alone all the time, but it was usually at my desk while I was working or fast food in the car while I was on the way from one job to the next. Melody never struck me as the kind of woman who'd do that. She had a lot of girlfriends according to Samantha, and she was always going somewhere to meet them for a drink or a movie or a party or even to work out together. That's why I'd thought she'd met some of her girlfriends at the cafe.

But if she'd met friends, wouldn't they have left together? Women tended to do things in groups. They went to the restroom together, gathered together at parties while the husbands and boyfriends they'd come with were off in another room talking business or watching the game on TV. Even as anti-social as I could be at times, when I'd been married to Ryan, I did the same thing.

No, if Melody had met with a group of girlfriends for lunch, they would have left the cafe together, or at least within a short span of time after Melody. That hadn't happened. The only person who came out of the cafe immediately after her had been Justin Sewell.

Had he been the person she'd met for lunch?

I zoomed out on the picture and studied it again, trying to figure out if I was reading more into her smile than was really there.

Melody had never struck me as a stupid woman. She was

engaged to a well-known local attorney. The cafe on California Avenue was only a few blocks away from the courthouse. All the cafes and restaurants in the area catered to the attorneys whose offices were clustered around the courthouse. Hell, Ryan's office was less than a quarter mile away. If Melody was going to have an affair with someone, even flirt with someone over lunch, she couldn't have chosen a worse place if she wanted to keep the whole thing a secret from Ryan.

But what if she hadn't cared? I couldn't tell from the picture whether she had her engagement ring on. In the shot, her left hand had been hidden from view when she turned to look at Justin.

I scrolled through a few more pictures in the sequence, trying to see if she had her engagement ring on, but none of the shots showed her clearly enough for me to tell.

I sat back in my chair, staring at my laptop but not really seeing it. What had she been up to? Had she been cheating on Ryan, or was it just an innocent lunch with her banker? Justin's business card did say that he was a *personal* banker. But why would Melody need to have lunch with a banker? As far as I knew, she had no plans to start a business of her own. Then again, I'd probably be the last person to hear if she did.

My cell phone vibrated. I'd put it on the table next to my laptop and turned the sound off so that if anyone called, the ringtone wouldn't wake Samantha. The house was still quiet, with only the sounds of the neighborhood filtering in. The occasional car passing on the street in front of the house, birds chattering in the trees, a neighbor mowing the lawn before the midday heat set in, someone else using a leaf blower to clean their yard by blowing the trash into someone else's.

In my neighborhood, life went on as usual. Melody's hadn't, but the neighborhood didn't care. There was probably a deep philosophical lesson in there somewhere, but I was too tired and too focused to worry about the big picture.

I glanced at my phone. I'd received a text from Kyle.

*You awake? I'm out front. Didn't want to knock if you're still sleeping.*

Instead of replying to the text, I padded over to my front door on bare feet. I unlocked the deadbolt and the security screen door and went out onto the front stoop.

Kyle had parked his unmarked police car in front of Freddie March's house. He must have seen me come out the door, because the next thing I knew he'd trotted across my front lawn and enveloped me in a hug.

"I was on a stakeout last night. I didn't hear about what happened until I got back to the station this morning and got your message," he said. "Are you all right?"

I shook my head. "Not even close."

He felt warm and solid in my arms. He smelled like coffee and cigarettes. Kyle didn't smoke, but he wasn't always alone on stakeouts. His normally clean-shaven cheeks were scratchy with stubble. I tilted my head back and saw the dark circles beneath his eyes.

"Catch your guy?" I asked.

"Made some progress."

He couldn't talk about specifics, and I knew better than to ask. When we did talk about his work, it was always in generalities.

"Are you sure you should be seen with me?" I said. "I'm a 'person of interest' in a homicide. Might not be good for your career."

The words came out sounding more bitter than I'd intended.

He snorted. "They're fishing, and they know it."

Kyle kissed me lightly on the lips, a gesture meant more to reassure than anything else, but I took it. After all of Norton's warnings about how serious my situation was, it was nice to get that reassurance even though I could tell by Kyle's expression that he was worried about me.

"Let's go inside," he said. "We've got some stuff to talk about."

I heard the sound of the shower when we went back inside. Samantha apparently couldn't sleep well, either.

During the entire summer, I'd rarely seen her up before ten-thirty in the morning, which meant that most days I was out of the house while she was still in bed. She was old enough that I trusted her to stay home alone, and not invite Maddie over if I said not to. I'd only taken her to the Marches' last night because the last thing I'd wanted was for my daughter to be alone after hearing that the woman who was about to become her step-mother had been murdered.

I poured Kyle a glass of iced tea and we sat at my dining room table. A picture I'd taken of Justin Sewell was still on my laptop screen.

"One of the guys I thought might be stalking Melody," I said, gesturing at the screen. "Now I'm not so sure."

While Kyle sipped his tea, I scrolled back through the pictures to the one of Melody looking back at the cafe, smiling at Sewell.

"She knows him," Kyle said. "Did she have lunch with him?"

"I'm starting to think that." I gave him a brief rundown on how I'd tracked Sewell back to the bank and got his name. "He's a personal banker. He didn't take my twenty bucks, so I'd thought he was an honest guy. Now I'm beginning to wonder."

"He could still be an honest guy, just an honest guy interested in a woman who isn't."

I didn't say anything about Kyle's present-tense reference to Melody. He'd only met her once. A few months after we'd started dating, we had a Friday night dinner date which we were late for because Ryan had been late picking up Samantha for the weekend. I never made Samantha wait at home by herself for her father, so the three of us had been watching a movie when Ryan eventually arrived with Melody, who'd either been drunk or high. She'd apologized for making Ryan late, and generally been much more charming than her usual sober self. She'd even flirted a bit with Kyle, which I'd figured was just because she hadn't been herself.

Or had she? Was she one of those women who had no boundaries? She'd told me once that she didn't know Ryan was married when they first started going out, but what if that had been a lie?

Kyle tapped some keys on the laptop, scrolling back and forth between the pictures I'd taken. "You have pictures of the guy you think is Richards on here?"

"Keep scrolling forward. The only good pictures I got of him were later, after I ran into Melody at the gym."

Instead of scrolling all the way to the end, he took his time looking at each picture I'd taken. The ones of the white SUV pulling out onto the street and driving past where I had been parked were blurry. If I hadn't run into Mr. Muscles at the gym, and then seen him go out to the SUV, I wouldn't have been able to find out who'd been driving just from the pictures I'd taken.

"Who's this?" Kyle asked, pointing at the screen.

The shot must have been taken right after the SUV passed my car. The SUV was a white blur off to the left side of the frame. I hadn't really studied the shot before since it didn't seem to be important.

Kyle was pointing at the older guy who'd been sitting by himself at the table for two in front of the cafe. The guy I'd thought had been annoyed when Justin Sewell was standing on the sidewalk taking cell phone pictures of Melody.

"He was eating lunch by himself while he was reading something on his tablet," I said. "I only noticed him because he looked pissed off when Justin got in his personal space."

In the shot, the guy wasn't looking at Justin. He was looking across the street toward the area where I had parked.

"How do you make this thing zoom in?" Kyle asked.

I worked the controls, and the guy's picture enlarged just like Melody's had.

"He made you," Kyle said.

Sure enough, once the picture was big enough and focused on the random diner, I could see that the guy was looking directly at the camera. Which meant he'd been looking at me.

"He must have seen the camera," I said. I'd been fairly subtle with the camera when I'd been trying to get a picture of Justin Sewell. The SUV had startled me enough that I'd forgotten to be covert. I'd just raised the camera and fired off shot after shot hoping that a picture would show me who was driving the car.

Kyle scrolled backwards through the pictures. This time I focused on the man sitting by himself at the table. He wasn't in many of the shots. Except for one early shot I'd taken of Justin before I'd tried to zoom in on his face, the man hadn't paid attention to anything except his tablet. In that early picture, he'd been looking at Justin, an expression of annoyance clear on his face.

"You think he's important?" I asked Kyle.

"I think he's familiar."

"Bad guy familiar?"

"Maybe." He spent another minute staring at the guy's picture before he shook his head. "It'll come to me," he said.

"In the shower."

He raised an eyebrow.

"That's where things I'm trying to remember come to me," I said. "In the shower, or in the middle of the night when I can't sleep."

"Or on stakeouts."

He rolled his shoulders like he was trying to stretch out stiff muscles. I'd been on a few stakeouts myself, waiting for hours in a car for a witness trying to duck a subpoena. I rubbed his shoulder, and he leaned into my touch.

"You're good at that," he said.

"Years of practice."

Kyle wasn't a big man, but he was solid. He worked out just enough to keep himself in the kind of shape he needed to be in to run down a suspect. The first time I'd slept with him, I'd been pleasantly surprised to discover that he didn't have six-pack abs.

Ryan was one of those men who was naturally athletic and built, and he had to do very little work to keep his six pack in perfect shape.

I wasn't naturally athletic, and even though I was trim enough, I'd always felt a little inferior in the body department compared to Ryan. With Kyle, I felt like we matched.

The relationship was still too new to figure out where it was headed, but I had a good feeling about us. I might even learn to like baseball.

As I rubbed his shoulders, Kyle scrolled forward through the pictures, not slowing down until he got to the pictures of Mr. Muscles that I'd taken while I was waiting in line to put gas in my car. He studied the last picture, one where I'd zoomed in on Mr. Muscles' face.

"That's him," he said after a moment. "Lewis Richards. Bulked up and a few years older, but that's the guy. He's bad news."

I stopped rubbing. "What kind of bad news?"

The shower had stopped running. I heard the bathroom door open. Samantha, headed back to her room. Once she was dressed, she'd be out in the kitchen, rummaging through the fridge for something that had the fewest possible calories for breakfast.

"Not the kind of news she should hear," Kyle said.

I closed the picture file and shut down my laptop. It wasn't too hot outside yet. We could sit outside and discuss the kind of things Kyle didn't want to mention around my daughter.

Two outdoor conferences in two days. The way things were going lately, maybe I shouldn't have let Ryan take all the good outdoor furniture with him when he moved out.

# 16

I wasn't sure I liked the idea of my backyard becoming the place I went to talk with people about unpleasant things. The memory of the discussion I'd had with the detectives the night before was still too strong, but at least Kyle wasn't here to arrest me. Not that I'd technically been under arrest, just the next best thing.

Kyle sat beside me on the glider, his arm around me, my head on his weary shoulder. The glider was still in the shade, so I wasn't in danger of burning the pale skin on my legs.

I'm not a sun worshipper like my neighbor. The couple who lived in the house on the other side of mine were in their late twenties, had no kids, and were gone most weekends. When they were home, she liked to sit out in the sun on a chaise lounge in the backyard, country music playing on a portable stereo. She was the tannest woman I'd ever seen. I wondered sometimes if she realized what her skin would look like in another twenty or thirty years.

My neighbor wasn't out in her yard this morning. The leaf blower had gone quiet, but another lawn mower had started up somewhere a few blocks over. A dove sat on the power line that ran down the backyard fence line between the houses on my block and the ones the next block over. It cooed at another dove hidden in the full branches of a tall Ponderosa pine that shaded the back corner of my yard.

"So tell me about Lewis Richards," I said.

We swung gently back and forth for a moment before Kyle responded.

"A lot of this comes from the guy I was on stakeout with last night. He used to work in the gang unit until he got assigned to Robbery/Homicide. He was part of a county-wide task force, one of those inter-agency, we're-better-off-pooling-our-resources things."

"He knew Richards?"

"He didn't work with him directly, but gangs and drugs go hand in hand, and he'd been given a heads up about Richards in case he ran into him in connection with his work."

Richards had apparently been the kind of undercover cop —at least back in those days—who immersed himself completely in the role. While no one ever proved it, everyone thought the way he got in close with the major drug dealers was by using whatever drug they happened to be selling.

"My guess is that his captain chose to look the other way," Kyle said. "I suppose I can understand it, from his perspective. Richards had an impressive track record. His information was responsible for putting a bunch of drug dealers behind bars."

"Wouldn't the bad guys eventually make the connection to him?" I asked.

"If he was sloppy, sure, but from what this guy told me last night, Richards wasn't sloppy. He had a network of informants who didn't have a clue they were passing along information to a cop. They thought they were just flying high with a fellow druggie, telling stories while they passed around the bong or snorted lines or did whatever other drug they were sharing. In a way I can admire the guy. It takes a certain level of focus to keep your head in a situation like that, and Richards had been on the job for years."

"Had been?"

"He was suspended six months ago. The press never got wind of it, not like when an officer's involved in a shooting, and the department kept it quiet, but apparently Richards was told to clean up his act or he'd be out for good."

I wondered if that's when he became Mr. Muscles. Spent all his time at the gym working out to get the drugs out of his system. Either that, or he'd replaced street drugs with steroids. One thing I knew about chronic steroid users was that they could have short tempers.

"I saw him arguing with Melody yesterday," I said. "You think he could have had anything to do with what happened to her?"

Kyle shrugged. "My guy said department gossip pegged Richards as a hothead, that he either mouthed off to his handler or belted the guy when he didn't like what he was getting told, so yeah, I guess it's possible."

"It's a lot more probable than Ryan torching Melody's car while she was inside."

"Where did they find the car?"

"I don't know exactly. All the cops mentioned was that it was in some vacant lot downtown and that someone passing by called it in. Norton might know. Or it might be on the news. I haven't checked this morning."

I hadn't wanted to look at the news. I'd been too afraid to see my picture or Ryan's mentioned in connection with Melody's murder.

Kyle stretched out his back, and I heard his jaw creak as he yawned.

"You should go home," I said. "You're exhausted."

His arm tightened around me. "I don't want to leave you alone today."

"Because you think I'm an emotional wreck, or because you're afraid I'm going to keep investigating this?"

He kissed me on the top of my head. "A little of both, but more because I'm worried you're in over your head and you haven't realized it yet."

A ginger cat hopped up on the back fence and walked along the top of the boards that gave me a little privacy from my neighbors. The dove on the power line tilted its head and gave the cat a beady-eyed stare, secure in the knowledge that it was out of the cat's reach.

"He's always going to be my daughter's dad," I said. "I can't just stand by and not do anything."

Kyle sighed. "I know. That's why I debated whether to tell you about Richards, but I figured you'd find out on your own anyway. These people are dangerous. Even if he didn't do it, the people he's run with are more than capable of killing someone just to send a message."

"But why kill Melody to send a message to Richards? She'd have to be someone important to him for that to matter."

Which brought me back to the question of why an undercover—former undercover—cop would be tailing her. What in the world did Melody have to do with any of that?

I didn't know, but I sure as hell was going to find out.

amantha decided to call her dad around noon. I wasn't surprised when the call went straight to his voicemail.

I tried not to listen in, but the house was still quiet. Kyle had gone home to sleep, and I'd been pretending to read a book in the den, but all I was doing was reading the same paragraph over and over again because the words refused to make sense.

Samantha cried a little, her voice thick, when she left a message for her dad telling him how sorry she was about Melody, that she loved him, and that she wanted to help if there was anything she could do. After she was done, she asked me if she could call Jonathan, and when I said yes, she took her cell phone into her room and shut the door.

I had a feeling it was going to be a long call, so I powered up my laptop again. I had work to do.

Ryan had suspected that Melody had a stalker, and the evidence he'd told me about had sure pointed in that direction. I had no proof that the stalker was the same person who'd murdered her, but I had no proof that he wasn't, either.

Kyle and Norton were both right, too. I couldn't investigate her murder the way I usually went about most investigations—by going backwards from the incident. Not only did the police have access to reports and data and investigation techniques that I didn't, if I butted in on their investigation, I'd just end up in jail for real on a charge of obstruction. I was better off concentrating on the stalker. At least it gave me a place to start.

According to Ryan, Melody's stalker had started by sending her flowers. A single red rose a day for a week to her at work.

Melody hadn't wanted to talk to Ryan about the roses. Okay, fine. But the roses had to come from somewhere.

Like a grocery store.

A guy could buy a single red rose along with a loaf of bread and a stick of salami at any number of grocery stores around town, but if that's where the roses came from, the guy who bought them would either have to deliver them in person or make arrangements for someone else to do it. If the women at the gym were like women everywhere, a red rose a day would get noticed.

So would whoever delivered it.

Stacy, the fashion-model thin woman behind the front desk at the gym, struck me as the kind of person who'd pay attention to a man who'd make that kind of romantic gesture, whether the gesture was wanted or not. If the roses had been delivered by a florist, she might even remember which one. The only way to find that out was to talk to her, something I wasn't looking forward to.

If a florist was involved, they might have a record of who bought the roses. Even if the guy paid in cash, a lot of retail stores had video cameras trained on the cash register. I couldn't compel them to let me look at surveillance tapes, but I'm pretty good at talking people into showing me what I needed to see.

Most days, anyway. Today I might look a little too stressed around the edges to carry off my normal, easy-going, you-can-tell-me-anything manner.

Of course, if the guy had used a bunch of different florists, it would take me a lot more time. I might be able to cut that time down if I contacted the florists by phone first instead of paying each of them a visit.

Speaking of phone calls, Ryan had told me that after the roses stopped, the stalker had moved up to harassing calls to the house and no doubt to Melody's cell as well. Ryan had told me the caller ID on those calls had been blocked.

The cops might be able to trace those calls. I couldn't. I'm not a computer hacker and I don't have any contacts who could get me information like that.

Even if I knew what phone company to check. I had no clue who Ryan's telephone service provider was, and Melody's cell probably burned up along with her car. Besides, if the stalker was smart, he would have used a prepaid phone and then dumped it. From my perspective, trying to track the phone calls was a dead end.

So were the photographs. Ryan had told me that Melody destroyed them. Nothing for me to track there.

Or was there? Justin Sewell had clearly been taking pictures of Melody with his cell phone. What if Sewell had taken the pictures Ryan saw? If he had, he could have been the guy on the phone as well, the one who'd hung up whenever Ryan answered. Was that why Melody told Ryan she was used to dealing with unwanted attention from men, because she knew Sewell was the guy making the phone calls and she'd just assumed he'd taken the pictures, too?

But then what about the roses? Had she assumed they'd come from Sewell as well?

Come to think of it, how had Ryan even found out about the roses if they'd been delivered to Melody at work?

I should have asked him back when we first discussed the whole thing, but I'd been too surprised by his request to really think through everything I might need to know. I couldn't ask him now since I wasn't supposed to be talking to him, and I sure as hell wasn't going to make Samantha be the go-between on something like that.

It seemed from the photo I'd taken that the attention Sewell had been showering on Melody wasn't exactly something she hated. From Ryan's perspective, she'd attracted a stalker. Maybe what she'd really attracted was a new boyfriend, and she didn't care if one of Ryan's friends found out.

I needed more information on Sewell, so I did a quick background check.

Born in Boca Raton, Florida, Justin Sewell was thirty-eight years old. He'd worked for his current bank for the last four and a half years, which was how long he'd lived in Reno. Before that, he'd been employed by a series of mortgage brokerages in Southern California.

The addresses where he'd lived since he'd come to Reno were all apartment buildings or condos, and it seemed like he bounced from place to place every six months. He had a modest bank account, an unremarkable credit history, no bankruptcies, he owned no property, and he had one car registered to his name, a three year old Prius. He'd never been married, and he had no litigation history in the court records I could access online. His parents were both deceased, and I could find no record of any siblings.

I was much more social media savvy now than I'd been last year when Samantha had introduced me to the world of blogging. These days I included searches of all major social media sites whenever I did a background check.

Justin Sewell had a LinkedIn profile, which was nothing more than typical banking promotional material. If he had a Facebook account, it wasn't under his own name. Ditto for Twitter and Pinterest.

Sewell was a big fat nothing online. If he was a player, he didn't talk about it and no one else talked about him. Even a

Google Images search on the name resulted in nothing except a picture of a smiling farmer in his eighties who'd grown a record-setting pumpkin a few years back.

The only thing out of the ordinary about Sewell was that he changed addresses frequently. Then again, he'd seemed to be new at that particular branch of his bank, so maybe he hopped from branch to branch every six months or so and just moved to be closer to his work. The address for his current apartment was near Reno High, only a couple of miles away from the branch where he worked.

The other way to get a handle on whether Melody knew Sewell as more than just a casual lunch date was to see what I could find online about her. I'd never bothered to look her up before, not even when Ryan and I had first split up. Back then my ego couldn't have handled it. Now I didn't have a choice.

Unlike Justin, Melody was all over the social media sites. She had a LinkedIn profile as a personal trainer, complete with a photo of her in skin-tight lavender leotards. She had a Twitter feed, although she didn't seem to post there often, unlike Facebook where I found multiple posts per day and more photographs than I had on my thumb drive.

The majority of the photographs were selfies. I felt ghoulish as I scrolled through picture after picture taken by a smiling, happy woman who'd pointed her cell phone camera at her own face, recording each happy day, blissfully unaware that her life was almost over. She'd taken some of the pictures in the foyer at the gym. I recognized the rock wall behind her. She'd snapped others at different nightclubs or restaurants around town, only some of which looked familiar.

Then there were the pictures she'd taken of herself with her friends. Stacy from the gym was in a few of the pictures with Melody. One picture showed Melody with a group of women, all wearing paper party hats and blowing noisemakers. The date the picture had been posted was last New Year's Eve. The caption below the picture identified the women by name: Melody, Stacy, Meghan, Gloria, and big sis Naomi.

I'd never known Melody had a sister. The resemblance was obvious, although Naomi's hair was a shade darker blonde and she had maybe ten pounds or so on Melody, a difference that was only noticeable because her cheekbones weren't quite as defined as her sister's. The picture had been taken at a private party—I could see a living room couch and a flat screen television in the background with the Times Square ball slowly descending toward the new year—but the one thing I didn't see in the picture was Ryan.

In fact, Ryan wasn't in any of the pictures on Melody's Facebook. Most of the pictures were of Melody alone or Melody with her girlfriends. No LOL cats or cute dogs, funny cartoons or memes, another term I'd learned from Samantha.

I scanned Melody's Facebook wall as far back as the program would let me. Whenever she made an actual post that wasn't a picture, it was about the fun she'd had the night before or a great new clothes shop she'd discovered or the smoothie she couldn't believe was low calorie because it just tasted so good.

Not one mention of Ryan anywhere, which made me wonder if that was Melody's decision, or his.

Ryan had worked hard to build a reputation as a quality attorney. The website for his law firm oozed solid professionalism from every pixel. None of the partners in the firm were over fifty, but the website was so old school that I always expected to see a picture of John Houseman on the home page.

The firm had hired a media consultant to spruce up their internet presence back when we'd still been married. I used to tease Ryan about the difference between his real personality—former college jock who still played every sport like he was going for the gold—and the calm, competent, professional persona he was trying to convey. He'd told me that flamboyant personalities went hand in hand with criminal law, but in order to attract business clients, the ones with deep pockets who could afford to pay their legal fees, he had to appear more serious than he really was.

Image gets them in the door, he'd said. From there, it was up to him to keep them from walking back out again. If all of that meant he had to act more dignified than he really was, so be it.

If Melody was really the party girl her online persona portrayed, that wouldn't have fit with the brand Ryan had worked so hard to create for himself. I could just imagine the discussions he'd had with her about what he did and did not want her posting as far as he was concerned.

But did that explain why Melody hadn't included a relation-ship status on her Facebook page?

Ryan had his own Facebook account. Just like the firm's website, Ryan's Facebook was subdued to the point of being downright staid. Melody could have mentioned that she was engaged to Ryan Maxon and left it at that. She hadn't.

Then again, when I clicked over the Ryan's Facebook page for a quick look, I noticed that he hadn't indicated a relation-ship status either.

Maybe teenagers were the only ones who did that.

But were teenagers the only ones who looked at Facebook to determine if someone was single? If Justin Sewell had looked up Melody on Facebook, he might have assumed she was avail-able. And if she accepted the roses he sent, talked to him on the phone, and agreed to meet him for lunch and flirted with him after she left, didn't that point to an affair in the making rather than a stalker?

I clicked back to the picture of Melody and the other women taken on New Year's Eve.

Ryan had told me they were going to a party at a colleague's house. At the time I'd been nursing a separated shoulder and living with Samantha in a rented condo while Norton Green-burger was having the crime scene my house had become cleaned so that Samantha and I could move back home. Ryan had been more attentive to me during that whole time than he'd been since we'd been divorced, and because of that, he'd been sure that I knew what his plans were for New Year's Eve.

Ryan should have been in that picture with Melody.

I knew what he was like. He just didn't decide a day or two before Valentine's Day to pop the question. He would have known, even back then, that he loved this woman enough to marry her. Hell, he'd loved her enough to break his daughter's heart when he'd left us for her.

Of all of the pictures on Melody's Facebook, he should have been in this damn picture. So why wasn't he?

Something was stabbing me in the hand. I looked down and realized that I'd clenched my fingers into such a tight fist my nails were digging into my palm.

I was furious, and worse than that, I was furious with a dead woman. She'd hurt the man some part of me would always love. She'd died and left him alone and broken, and I couldn't fix it.

It wasn't logical to be angry at her because she was dead, so I'd shifted the focus of my fury to some imagined slight because he'd been left out of this picture. But why did I assume he'd been left out on purpose? For all I knew, he'd been watching a football game with the guys in another room or taking a bathroom break or been doing any one of a million other things. He could have been the one taking the picture, for god's sake, since this one wasn't a selfie.

I slammed the laptop closed more forcefully than the poor machine deserved.

I had to get a grip. Norton and Kyle were right. I had no business working this case, not if I couldn't keep a lid on my emotions.

I'd only stepped away from a case once in my life, and it had been because my emotions wouldn't let me see straight. I still had a file in my desk drawer at the office where I'd stuffed all the work I'd done trying to find the hit and run driver who'd nearly killed my daughter. Norton would have called that file my albatross. I thought of it as my white whale.

I didn't need a second white whale in my life. Especially not one of my own making.

I took a deep breath and opened the laptop, and went back to work.

## 18

I got the first glimmer that I might be suited to life as a private detective when I was college. I'd uncovered the identity of the thief who stole my wallet through a bit of deductive reasoning, some legwork, and a bit of luck, with an assist from Ryan and his friend, Jimmy Fisher.

That had brought me to the attention of Ed Hastings, then a detective with the Reno Police Department. Ed told me I had a talent for detective work and if I ever thought I might like to pursue a career in law enforcement, to give him a call.

Ryan and I got married in a church in downtown Reno during our senior year at the University of Nevada-Reno. After we graduated, Ryan enrolled in McGeorge School of Law, and we both moved to Sacramento. I lost track of Ed, although I never threw out his business card.

The three years Ryan and I lived in Sacramento while he attended law school and I waited tables at a restaurant near the campus convinced us both that we had no desire to make California our home. We returned to Reno where Ryan went to work as a very junior associate at an insurance defense firm and I found myself in need of a real job to augment Ryan's very junior salary.

I remembered Ed, but when I called the number on his card, I discovered that he'd retired from the force soon after we met and started his own agency. Just as well. I've never been a fan of guns. Although Ed had mentioned that detectives handled white collar investigations, I knew I'd still have to become a cop, complete with gun, before I could work my way up to a detective's shield.

Ed's experience as a cop enabled him to get a private investigator's license, and he was also licensed to serve process for the courts and private attorneys. The only work experience I had was refilling customers' drinks and making sure I didn't trip with their food before I had a chance to serve it.

To get my own investigator's license, I needed to apprentice with a licensed private investigator. Ed agreed to take me on at a salary that made Ryan's look majestic by comparison.

What I didn't earn in wages I more than made up for in experience.

Ed turned out to be the best mentor I could have asked for. I learned more about the world from him than I did from all the classes I'd taken in college, but he was more than just a teacher.

Ed pulled waiting room duty at the hospital when I gave birth to Samantha, and he nearly killed Ryan when he shoved a lit cigar in my then-husband's unsuspecting mouth to celebrate our new arrival. He taught me the value of play-acting when trying to serve a witness who didn't want to be found. He even knew when it was time to kick me out of the nest so I could start my own business.

When Ed died of cancer after a long and happy life spent smoking the cigars he knew would eventually kill him, I felt like I'd lost my best friend.

One of Ed's favorite sayings had been "trust your instincts."

What my instincts were telling me now was that Lewis Richards was a dirty cop.

Kyle hadn't come right out and said that. In fact, all he'd said was that Richards was a hothead and he'd been told to clean up his act, the implication being that all the drugs Richards had taken while he was undercover finally got to him, and it was time to admit he was an addict and get some help.

I wasn't naive enough to think that just because a cop had a drug problem, he had to be dirty. Some highly-regarded attorneys I'd met when I'd been married to Ryan were battling substance abuse problems of their own.

Litigators were Type A personalities for the most part who worked in a high-stress environment. Drug addiction wasn't uncommon, even among judges. For most alcohol was the drug of choice. Not surprising in a town like Reno where the casinos and bars and liquor stores never seemed to close.

For some, though, the drugs they abused—heroin and cocaine and designer drugs that changed street names as fast as they changed chemical compounds—were only available from dealers or junkies or people with the wrong kind of connections. Professionals, if they wanted to stay professionals, at least managed to stay away from meth.

I wondered if Richards had, since when Kyle had busted him, he'd described Richards as a skinny little prick. The few meth heads I'd had the unfortunate pleasure of running into during my process serving career had all been skinny as a rail with bad teeth, bad complexions, and bad attitudes.

No, it wasn't the drugs that made me think Richards was dirty. It was the way he'd smiled at me when he took my picture outside Melody's gym. Like he'd just learned my worst secret and couldn't wait to use it against me.

After I cleared my browser's history of the research I'd done on Melody—I didn't really need to save anything that I'd learned on her Facebook page—I ran a background check on Lewis Richards.

I wasn't surprised to find very little information.

At first glance, his current address looked like an apartment building, but I recognized the address as a mail drop where the apartment numbers were really post office boxes. He had no current credit history. The few credit cards he'd had at one time had all been closed, and the loan for the white SUV had been paid off early. He had no bank accounts in his name, had never filed for bankruptcy, and the only court history was a fifteen year old divorce case that looked like it had breezed through the courts without a hitch.

According to the court docket, his ex-wife's name was Gloria and she hadn't been represented by an attorney during the divorce.

On a whim, I ran a search on Gloria Richards. It apparently wasn't an uncommon name, and I came up pages and pages of hits for women that might have been Richards' ex. Without further information, I couldn't be sure, and I wasn't going to get the kind of information I needed from Richards' background check. His wife's name hadn't been on any of the few credit accounts he'd had when he'd been married.

I scrolled through the first few pages to see if any references to Gloria Richards caught my eye. I quit scrolling when I hit a link for a news story out of Boca Raton, Florida.

Boca Raton. That was where Justin Sewell came from.

The coincidence was too weird not to look. I clicked on the link, but instead of a webpage, I got a page not found error message. Undeterred, I checked to see if I could find a cached version of the webpage the link pointed to.

I got lucky. The image links were broken but the text of the article was still there.

*Antonio "Gordo" Gordino Makes Waves*

*Long-time Boca Raton resident Antonio "Gordo" Gordino returned home Friday afternoon following an extended stay up north courtesy of the federal government.*

*As previously reported, Mr. Gordino had been held without bail awaiting trial on charges of racketeering, money laundering, and tax evasion.*

*When all charges were abruptly dropped, Mr. Gordino was released from custody Thursday morning. Federal prosecutors declined to comment when asked why the charges were dismissed.*

*Asked the same question, Mr. Gordino simply replied that it was good to be home.*

*Employees at the Boca Bay Breakers might not be so happy to have the boss back in town. Inside sources tell this reporter that Mr. Gordino, who purchased a controlling interest in the resort hotel two years ago, made a clean sweep of all upper management personnel upon his return.*

*"We're moving ahead in a bold new direction in keeping with the new century," said the Breakers' Public Relations manager Gloria Richards.*

*While Ms. Richards did not confirm the ouster of CEO Phillip Conroy and CFO Walden Spears, she stated that the Breakers would be expanding, adding attractions and amenities that would not only increase the number of tourists expected to visit the resort but benefit residents of the community as well.*

*"We're very excited," she said.*

*The expansion of the Breakers might draw sharp opposition from the city council...*

The rest of the article dealt with local politics and the city's strict development code, which regulated the size of commercial buildings within the city limits. While fascinating reading, it was a rabbit hole I didn't want to go down.

The original article was published in a local paper in May of 2001. Could that Gloria Richards have been Lewis Richards' ex-wife?

I searched combining Richards and Gordino, but all I got were a few more hits to cached pages detailing the progress of the resort's expansion.

A resort owned by a mobster.

I spent a little time searching for information on Antonio Gordino. I wanted to know if he had any ties to Nevada, specifically to northern Nevada.

From what I found, he appeared to be strictly an east coast wiseguy. He was still alive and kicking back in Boca Raton. No other federal cases had been brought against him, and it looked like even the tax evasion charge had gone away.

He had two daughters by two different wives, and a couple of grandkids. Neither the daughters nor the wives were named Gloria. He operated the Breakers under a couple of different holding companies owned by other holding companies owned by trusts and LLCs.

The paper trail wasn't just a rabbit hole, it was a maze, and I had to draw a diagram to keep it all straight. Eventually the paper trail pointed back to Gordino. Complex and convoluted, yes, but if the feds hadn't been able to make a case against him stick, it was probably all legal.

I was about to close out the browser windows I had open when something made me go back to the organizational documents for one of the LLCs.

The members of the LLCs were more LLCs except for one —Widows and Orphans of Southern Florida Irrevocable Trust Dated June 26, 1982.

I'd seen the name of that trust before.

I opened up the background check I'd run on Justin Sewell. In his LinkedIn Profile, he'd listed various charitable organizations for whom he'd done volunteer work in the past, some dating as far back as when he still lived in Florida. Locally he'd volunteered at the Food Bank and Habitat for Humanities. While the charities looked good on his resume, I wrote those off as "volunteer" work the bank required all its employees to do.

I'd first learned about mandatory volunteer work when I'd gone to a Relay for Life event once as a chaperone for Samantha and Maddie. I'd been surprised by the number of local businesses—especially banks—who'd shown up to support the event. I'd even spotted my favorite teller, a middle-aged woman named Debbie who had pictures of her Chihuahuas inside her window at the bank, working at the bank's tent along with a bunch of other people all wearing tee shirts advertising the bank's new loan programs.

I'd stopped by the tent to say hello, and I'd asked her who she was supporting in the relay since many of the teams in the relay ran in honor of a cancer survivor.

She'd given me a disbelieving stare. "I get six hours of community service for being here today. That's half my yearly quota. Don't get me wrong. I think this is a worthy charity and all, but I have two jobs and I like my Sundays off."

"At least we get paid for it now," another woman in one of the bank's tee shirts said.

All the business tents were set up on the grassy infield at a local high school track where the relay was being held. Some of the tents featured amateur carnival games, and others offered handmade trinkets for sale. I even saw a man making balloon animals for little kids. A fair amount of people staffed each of the tents, most wearing matching company tee shirts, and I saw more people wearing company tee shirts out walking the track.

"You mean everyone out here is conscripted help?" I asked.

"It's called public facing. The companies like the publicity, but they know they'd never get anyone to come out to these things if they didn't require us to 'volunteer,' so..." The woman shrugged. "At least this is a nice, low-key event, and there's not much work involved."

No kidding. I'd expected a regular relay race, with baton

passing and sprints for the finish line. It looked like anyone who wanted could walk on the track. Samantha and Maddie had walked a couple of laps before they retired to the bleachers where they could watch the boy who was the real reason they'd wanted to come here today.

"That's right," Debbie said. "I did an early Saturday morning shift at Habitat, and they had me hauling lumber and climbing in and out of a trench. This volunteer stuff was a whole lot easier back when they let us donate blood."

I didn't know for sure that the Food Bank was on the approved list of charities at Justin Sewell's bank, but I had an idea that if one bank wanted its employees to volunteer at Habitat for Humanities, his did too.

He listed the American Cancer Society and the Special Olympics as the charities where he'd volunteered when he'd been living in southern California. I scanned further down the list until I came to the name I was looking for.

When Justin Sewell had still been living in Florida, he'd done volunteer work with an organization called the Widows and Orphans of Southern Florida.

I sat back in my dining room chair, trying to make sense of what I'd just discovered pretty much by accident.

Justin Sewell had a connection to a charity with the same name as a trust that had an interest—several times removed, but still an interest—in a resort hotel in Boca Raton owned by an east-coast mobster.

A woman with the same name as Lewis Richards' ex-wife had worked at the same resort hotel. Not only worked there, but had managed to hold onto her job even after her boss fired pretty much all the rest of the existing management staff, right down to the guy in charge of employee parking. The clean sweep had made the local news for weeks.

That couldn't be a coincidence. Reno was a small town, but it wasn't that small.

I pulled up Justin Sewell's credit history and looked the report over again. The first time through I hadn't given much thought to the numbers except to note that he didn't seem to outspend his income or have a lot of extra cash in the bank.

This time I looked more closely.

I'm not an accountant by any stretch of the imagination. I didn't have the kind of training the cops who investigated white collar crimes had. Even Ryan knew when he was in over his head when it came to squeezing information out of the reams of accounting reports that flowed hot and heavy in the big business lawsuits he handled and it was time to call in a forensic accountant. All I had was common sense and that gut instinct Ed Hastings encouraged me to follow.

I looked up the apartment complexes where Sewell had lived during the time he'd been in Reno, this time with an eye toward the amount of the monthly rent.

The cost of living in Reno wasn't exactly cheap, and the apartment buildings Sewell had called home were on the high end, just shy of luxury.

Most of the complexes required one-year leases. Sewell had moved every six months, which meant he would have had to pay at least a penalty if not the remainder of the lease whether or not he lived there. That was a big chunk of money for a guy who was just a personal banker.

Plus, he probably hadn't started out at the bank as a personal banker, but rather as a teller.

I knew from talking to my favorite teller Debbie at the Relay for Life event that she had to work two jobs to make ends meet. Banks weren't notorious for over-paying their employees. Unless Sewell was raking in enormous sales bonuses, he had to have another source of income.

Something related to the Widows and Orphans of Southern Florida Trust?

I had just started to think about how I could figure that out when it hit me.

None of this mattered.

So what if the trust was paying him? It was an interesting theory, but what did it have to do with Melody? At best, it meant Sewell was getting a little extra disposable income for his past good deeds. He'd probably picked up the check for his lunch with Melody. He'd probably picked up a lot of checks for lunches and dinners and room service champagne for lots of pretty women over the years.

At worst it meant Sewell was laundering money for the mob.

Even if I confirmed that, which I doubted I could since the feds with all their manpower and experts couldn't make a charge of money laundering stick against Gordino, following the mob's money wasn't going to lead me to who'd killed Melody. I kind of doubted that a semi-retired east-coast mobster would order a hit on a personal trainer just because she'd had lunch with Sewell. Especially not a hit that would garner the attention of the press.

I'd let myself get off track.

If I really wanted to find the man who'd sent Melody roses, who'd taken pictures of her, who'd written her a note on one of those pictures telling her she was a bad girl because she'd been talking on her cell while she'd been driving, I'd have to go talk to her friends. See if any of them had noticed anything out of the ordinary. If they remembered who'd delivered the roses.

My subconscious knew it. I should have known that too, but I'd been stalling because I knew those conversations weren't going to be pleasant. I'd have to talk to people who were still in shock over her death. People who were grieving. People who knew Melody hadn't liked me, and who probably knew Ryan and I had both been interviewed by the police in connection with her death.

Well, I couldn't put it off any longer, not unless I wanted to waste more time tracking down some mysterious connection between Santa Claus and the Easter Bunny. It was time to go do one of the things I did best. Talk to people, and listen to what they had to say.

I was going to have to go visit Melody's friends at the gym.

## 19

Samantha hadn't been happy when I told her I had a little work I had to do.

I could have made things easier on myself if I'd explained to her about where I was going and why, but I didn't want her to know that the police suspected her dad was involved in Melody's murder. If it looked like the cops were going to arrest Ryan, we'd talk about it then.

Until that happened, Samantha had enough to deal with. In a couple more years she'd be eighteen and heading off to college. Right now she was still my baby girl, and I wanted to protect her. Although something told me I wouldn't be able to switch off the protective mom gene when she hit eighteen.

Stacy, the fashion-model thin receptionist at the gym where Melody had worked, apparently wasn't happy with me either. Her professionally pleasant expression hardened when she saw me walk through the gym's front door.

"Can I help you?" she said, but her tone made it clear helping me was the last thing she wanted to do.

Stacy had more than a couple of inches on me, and that was in tennis shoes. Still, I could see the puffiness around her eyes that her makeup couldn't quite mask and the tension lines at the corners of her mouth. The pictures I'd seen on Melody's Facebook made it clear that Stacy and Melody had been friends. Coming to work, knowing that Melody wouldn't be there—would never be there again—I'd come close to that kind of pain when Ed died.

I could relate to Stacy's pain. I just hadn't expected outright hostility, which made me wonder what Melody had said about me. Had she complained to Stacy about Ryan's shrewish ex-wife? Stacy hadn't known who I was when I came in yesterday. She knew now. This conversation was going to be harder than I'd thought, if she'd even talk to me.

"I'm very sorry for your loss," I said.

Her eyes welled up for a moment, and she gripped the edge of the black granite countertop so tight her knuckles turned white. She was holding herself together—barely. The last thing I wanted to do was make her break down while she was supposed to be the public face of the gym.

"Is there somewhere we can go to talk?" I asked.

Her chin rose just enough that she looked down her nose at me. The attitude adjustment must have been her way of holding back the tears. "I don't think so," she said. "I can't imagine what we'd have to say to each other."

I nodded, agreeing with her. "That's true. The only thing we have in common is Melody."

"You didn't have Melody." The words came out clipped. Angry.

I knew that anger was a part of grief. I'd just had my own bout of anger not that long ago. By showing up here today, I'd given Stacy a convenient target for hers. I could take bearing the brunt of her anger if she'd talk to me, but it would be easier on us both if I could find a way around it.

"She was part of my extended family," I said. "She was a part of my daughter's life. My daughter will never forget her."

"Your daughter didn't even like her. She told me your daughter quit talking to her after..." Her voice caught, and her eyes grew shiny again. I pretended not to notice.

"After Ryan proposed," I said. "He could have handled that a little better, I admit, but most children of divorce harbor a hope that their parents will quit being stupid and get back together. Samantha's no different. She didn't realize that was never going to happen."

Stacy gave me a sharp look. "Because Melody got in your way? Well, she'd not now."

What had Melody told this woman? Did she actually think I'd do something to Melody just to get Ryan back? And if she did, had she told the cops the same thing?

No wonder Archulette and Squires thought I was involved. It wasn't just because I'd been tailing Melody to find a stalker.

I couldn't defend myself. I'd be contradicting her friend, and her friend was dead.

"No, she isn't," I said. "And she should be. She should be alive to have the wedding of her dreams and long years of having fun with her friends and maybe having a few kids of her own. She should be taking all those fabulous trips with Ryan that he always used to talk about, see all the places in the world he wanted to visit only things always got in the way and he never had the time to go anywhere fabulous. I think he would have wanted to do that with her because she was young and energetic and beautiful, and he always seemed to have so much fun with her. Did I like that he had more fun with her than he'd had with me? Was I jealous? Yes, I was, but the fact of the matter was that Ryan loved her. She should have lived to have the life with him she wanted, but she won't, and I want to know why. Don't you?"

I hadn't intended for all of that to come spilling out, but I couldn't have stopped once I got started. I was still too angry myself.

By the time I was done, tears had spilled down Stacy's cheeks. She swiped at them with the back of her hand, then gave a quick sideways glance at the door to the workout rooms.

"Give me five minutes," she said. "I need to get someone to cover for me. Wait for me outside, and I'll come talk to you."

It took her ten minutes, and I'd almost thought she'd changed her mind.

I watched other people head into the gym—pony-tailed women who drove into the parking lot in BMWs and Lexus sedans and big Escalade SUVs, their gym clothes color-coordinated with their duffel bags or oversized purses; college-age jocks in sleeveless tee shirts and shorts, muscles bulging on their shoulders and arms and thighs, trying to keep themselves in shape for whatever college sport they played; even a few businessmen who wanted to work off the stress of their mornings. A group of young women came out, their hair still wet from showers, and I heard them chatting about daycare and potty training, and did they want to grab a skinny iced mocha before picking up the kids?

My stomach rumbled, reminding me that I hadn't had much to eat so far today. Or drink, for that matter.

The gas station across the parking lot was one of those gas station/mini-mart combination stores so popular these days. I could almost taste the iced tea I was sure they had in their self-serve machines.

The day had turned out to be another scorcher like the morning had promised, and I was beginning to regret that I hadn't worn a hat. The front of the gym faced south, and there was absolutely no shade to be found. I could feel my scalp burning along the part in my hair, to say nothing of my nose, and my deodorant had waved the white flag after the first couple of minutes of unrelenting sunshine.

When Stacy finally came outside, she was wearing wrap-around sunglasses, and she'd pulled a pair of short-shorts over her hot pink spandex leotard and leggings. She nodded her thanks to an older man who'd held the door open for her and another couple of women, all of them leaving the gym. The older guy had on dark glasses and a Reno Aces baseball cap, and he was the first one I'd seen dressed in a sensible plain white tee shirt and lightweight workout pants.

Something niggled at my brain about the older guy, but then Stacy walked over to me and I shifted my attention to her.

"Thank you," I said when she got close to me. I'd decided to wait off to the side of the gym. I didn't want to look like I was lurking, and besides, I thought Stacy might not want anyone inside to see who she was talking to.

"I only have a couple of minutes. We're short staffed today, otherwise I wouldn't be here."

The lenses of the sunglasses she wore were so dark, I couldn't see her eyes at all. It meant I wouldn't be able to read her expression as well as I could inside, but at least the sunglasses weren't mirrored. I wouldn't have to look at my sweaty, wilted reflection while I talked to her.

She sighed. "It feels wrong to be at work today."

I knew how she felt, but I wasn't going to say that. I'd managed to create a tenuous connection with Stacy by focusing on Melody, and that's where the focus needed to stay. And while I didn't have a lot of time, I couldn't just come right out and ask about the roses. I had to build up to that.

"About work," I said. "Did Melody ever have any trouble with anyone at the gym?"

Stacy shook her head. "The cops asked that. I told them no, and they looked at me like they didn't believe me. Everybody liked Melody."

I wondered if the cops who'd talked to her had been the same detectives who'd interviewed me. I hadn't come away with a very good impression of them either.

"What about the guy yesterday?" I asked.

"The guy who left his lights on?"

I nodded.

"He's okay. Kind of intense sometimes. Melody's helping... she was helping him develop a personalized workout routine. Guys like that who've been out of shape for a while, when they get the workout bug and decide they want a better body, they can overdo it. He was in here all the time, doing free weights, riding the elliptical. She was trying to get him to cut back, get him into a routine that would be better for his body."

She looked down at her feet. Her tennis shoes looked brand new. I couldn't remember the last time my tennis shoes had looked that clean.

"I probably shouldn't be telling you all this about a client," she said. "Melody said you're an investigator. Is that what you're doing? Investigating what happened to her? Working with those cops?"

"I'm not working with the cops, but I am going to find out what happened."

"I guess that means you don't trust them either." This time when she raised her head, I knew she was looking at me. "Good."

No, the cops hadn't made a very good impression on her at all.

"Anything else you can think of about this guy?" I asked.

She shrugged. "He flirted with her. I mean, a lot of the guys flirt with us. We're supposed to sell the sexy part of getting in shape, that's why we have to wear these." She gestured at her tight outfit. "And I thought being a cocktail waitress was bad. At least here I don't have to walk around in heels."

"Anybody ever try to get serious with the flirting?"

"Like what, try to date her?"

"Like that."

"She didn't cheat on Ryan, if that's what you're asking." The defensive tone had crept back into her voice.

"That's not what I'm asking. I'm just wondering if any of the guys who flirted with her saw the engagement ring as a challenge."

"Sometimes. Plus sometimes they didn't know she was engaged. She couldn't wear the ring when she was working with a client one-on-one. We can't wear jewelry then. It's against the rules. Nothing except a plain wedding band or simple stud earrings."

The ban made sense. I'd seen Melody's engagement ring. It was bigger than the ring Ryan had given me, but then again when we got married, he was still a struggling college student not a successful attorney.

"Any guy in particular you remember?" I asked.

She didn't answer right away. Either she was trying to remember or trying to decide whether to tell me. I didn't push her.

"Yeah," she finally said. "There was this one guy. Worked in a bank, I think. He only came in a couple of times, but he got real interested in Melody. Kept pestering her to come in and open an account."

Justin Sewell? "You remember his name?" I asked.

She shrugged. "He never signed up for a membership. We offer free passes. It lets people see if they'd like it here, plus people always like free stuff. The passes get them in the door, then it's up to the rest of us to give them a reason to want to come back."

That sounded like what I used to hear from Ryan about his website. It was all about image. I didn't do that with my own business. I'd always thought that doing the best job possible was what mattered, and word of mouth would keep me in business.

"He had a couple of passes. We usually only honor one per customer, but Melody let this guy use both of them." Stacy frowned a little at the memory. "He hit on her right away. She flirted back, but it was just to keep him interested in signing up for a membership."

I wondered if the people who worked at the gym got incentives for signing up new memberships. It wouldn't surprise me. A lot of service jobs were really sales jobs in disguise. Like personal bankers.

"Do you think he just wanted her to open an account or..."

I didn't think I had to spell it out. I didn't.

"Oh, he wanted her to open more than just an account." Stacy wrinkled her nose. "He was one of those kind of guys who thinks he's way more charming than he really is and can't understand why we all don't just jump into bed with him."

I had no doubt she'd encountered her fair share of men like that. Besides being fashionably thin, Stacy had the kind of doe-eyed, high-cheekboned beauty that was popular these days.

It bothered me that this was the ideal that teens like Samantha aspired to. Not everyone was meant to be this trim or have cheekbones that could cut glass. On Stacy, it looked natural and normal. Even in the pictures I'd seen of her on Melody's Facebook page, Stacy looked comfortable in her own skin just as it was. If that was true, she was a very rare woman indeed.

I wished I had a picture of Justin Sewell to show her, but all the pictures I'd taken were on my camera, and I'd been too distracted when I left the house to remember to put my camera in my purse.

"You remember what this guy looked like?" I asked. "White? Hispanic? Asian? Any visible tattoos?"

"White, I remember that, and no tattoos." She shrugged again. "He looked like somebody you'd see in an office, someplace that wants the guys in suits and ties and business haircuts, but nothing too high end that would put regular people off. He wasn't out of shape or anything either. Pleasant enough to look at, but I'm not sure I'd recognize him if I saw him on the street."

I found it fascinating what Stacy remembered about people. Not so much their physical features but what kind of impression their overall appearance made on other people. My overall appearance probably screamed frumpy. I decided I didn't want to hear what she'd remember about me.

She turned her head to look back at the gym. Probably checking to see if anyone was coming out to tell her that her little unscheduled break was over. Pretty soon she was going to tell me she had to get back to work, and I still didn't have everything I needed.

"Does the gym keep records of who uses the passes?" I asked. "Anything that would have this guy's name on it?"

"You think he had something to do with what happened?"

Now it was my turn to shrug. "I don't think anything yet."

Which wasn't exactly true, but most of what I thought I knew were unconnected pieces and random coincidences, nothing that formed a concrete pattern I could point to and say "that's the guy, not Ryan."

"Most of what I do involves asking questions," I said. "Sometimes the answers lead nowhere. Sometimes they lead to the next question, and if I'm lucky, somewhere down the line, I'll stumble on the right question and get the right answer."

She looked at me for a long moment. "That sounds..." She hesitated while she searched for the right word. "Frustrating."

"Serving court papers is easier," I said. "Unless the guy I'm trying to serve knows I'm coming and tries to duck me. Then it gets interesting."

Her cell phone chirped at her. She took it out of a pocket I hadn't noticed in her short-shorts and frowned at it. "I have to get back," she said. "Cici has a client coming in."

"About that name?" I asked.

"I'll look through the sign-in sheets, see if I can remember when he came in, but I can't guarantee anything. If I find something, I'll text you."

I gave her my cell phone number and watched while she typed it into her phone, her thumbs moving faster than I could type on my keyboard with two hands.

She was just about to the door when I remembered I hadn't asked the one question I really wanted an answer to. "Anybody ever send Melody flowers at work?" I said.

She paused with one hand on the door handle. "Besides Ryan?"

"Yes."

She shook her head. "Not that I know of."

"Red roses," I said. "A single rose a day for a week."

A frown creased her forehead. "She would have told me about that, or I would have heard from Cici. Unless they came from Ryan, but she still would have..." She shook her head again. "No. I'm sure she would have told me."

She disappeared inside the gym, leaving me with an even bigger question than the one I'd had to start out with.

## 20

I f Stacy had told me the truth, Melody had lied to Ryan about the roses. She didn't get them at work.

I'd given in to the need for a super-sized iced tea from the gas station/mini-mart. I sat in my hot car in the parking lot with all the windows rolled down and tried to figure out where to go from here.

The roses were a dead end. The only people who knew where Melody got the roses and who they were from were Melody and the person who'd given them to her.

I didn't know why she'd lied to Ryan about the roses in the first place. Based on my own experience, people in a relationship lied to either spare the other person's feelings or to hide something they were ashamed of. If she'd wanted to spare Ryan's feelings, she wouldn't have told him about the roses in the first place.

Did that mean she'd lied to hide something she was ashamed of? Like what?

Stacy was convinced Melody hadn't cheated on Ryan, and from what Melody had shared with the world on Facebook, it looked like Stacy was her best friend. So if she hadn't been cheating, what had she been ashamed of?

And why tell a lie that Ryan could have discovered on his own? I doubted Ryan was a stranger to the gym, and Stacy clearly knew him enough to be at least a little protective of her best friend's relationship with him. All Ryan had to do was mention the roses in casual conversation with someone at the gym and Melody's lie would fall apart.

Unless she'd wanted it to fall apart. Unless she was doing something she was so ashamed of that she subconsciously wanted Ryan to find out so that he'd make her stop, and the lie about the roses was an attempt at self-sabotage.

Okay, I was psychoanalyzing without a license. I was hot and tired and frustrated and making stuff up because I still couldn't see how all the puzzle pieces fit together.

I guzzled down a third of my iced tea, concentrating on nothing but the slightly bitter taste and how good it felt to hold the cold cup in my hands.

I'd given up using any kind of sweetener in my tea about the same time Samantha had started seriously counting calories. The stuff in the blue packets I used to add to my tea wasn't good for me, Samantha had informed me, and she wished I'd stop using artificial sweeteners at all. I told her that was fine, but she'd have to give up soda because that wasn't good for her, either. She'd said fine, and we'd struck a deal.

I wasn't sure what had been worse—her caffeine withdrawals or me getting used to the bitter taste of unsweetened iced tea. At least I didn't get headaches quite as often, so maybe it was a good thing after all.

After the iced tea helped me turn my inner Dr. Phil off, I thought about the information I had learned.

I knew more now than I had before about Lewis Richards and Justin Sewell. According to Stacy, both men had been interested in Melody, but her interest had been strictly business, even if part of that business was to sell the sex appeal of a well-toned body.

With Richards, Melody had been his personal trainer. I wondered for how long. Kyle had told me that Richards had been suspended for the last six months so he could get his life in shape. Apparently he'd taken that literally. Had he substituted one addiction for another? Maybe. Addicts could be unpredictable people, and she'd had confrontations with him about the best way to achieve the results he wanted.

But why had he been waiting for her outside the cafe? That couldn't have had anything to do with a disagreement over a workout routine. Richards had invaded her personal life, just like a stalker. Had his addiction to getting his body in shape morphed into an unhealthy obsession with his personal trainer?

I tried to remember whether I'd seen the white SUV earlier in the day when I'd been following Melody all over town so I could try to catch a glimpse of her stalker. I certainly didn't remember a white SUV taking off after her like Richards had when she'd left the cafe. I couldn't be sure if I'd seen him at any other time.

Richards had clearly seen Sewell come out of the cafe after Melody just like I had, and he'd probably had a better vantage point to see her turn around and give Sewell a flirty little come-hither grin. Richards had certainly pulled away from the curb in a hurry to follow her as she headed back to work, and he'd been upset enough that he'd had the angry conversation with her I'd witnessed over an hour later.

But was he angry enough to kill her? He hadn't seemed angry when he'd taken my picture with his cell phone outside of the gym. He'd seemed self-satisfied, somehow.

I didn't have enough information to take any of my suspi-

cions about Richards to the cops. I had a few facts, a few obser-
vations, but most of what I had was speculation, and it was
going to take more than speculation to turn the detectives'
interest away from Ryan and onto Richards.

And what if Richards wasn't the right guy? Justin Sewell
was still waiting in the wings.

I was pretty sure Sewell was the banker Stacy had been
talking about. A well-off middle class guy who'd wheedled an
extra free trip to the gym out of a woman he was flirting with.
Why had she agreed to have lunch with him? He didn't sound
like a guy who would spring for lunch if he wasn't getting
something in return.

I needed more information on Sewell. I could talk to his
neighbors, but a guy who moved every six months was a guy
who didn't make close ties to anyone in his neighborhood. He'd
moved from branch to branch within his own bank. The people
he worked with might know more about him, but if I had to
guess, I imagined that while he might be the subject of
company-wide gossip, I doubted any of his co-workers actually
knew very much about the real him.

I studied my reflection in the rearview mirror. My nose and
cheeks were a little on the pink side, but any real sunburn
wouldn't come out until after I showered.

Before I'd left the house, I'd changed out of the shorts I'd
worn that morning and put on a pair of jeans. Not designer
jeans by any stretch of the imagination, but new enough that
they'd be acceptable in a casual work environment.

My light-weight tee shirt was a little too casual, but I had a
white cotton button-front blouse in the backseat I could throw
on like an over-shirt, the summer equivalent of a suit jacket. I
didn't have strappy sandals in the car—I wasn't sure I had a pair
of strappy sandals in my closet either—so my tennis shoes
would have to do.

I could pull my hair back into a ponytail, wipe the sweat off my face with a little of the bottled water I always had in the car, and presto-chango—instant businesswoman off to meet with her brand new personal banker.

I just hoped he hadn't taken the day off.

# 21

Justin Sewell still occupied the same desk at the bank where I'd seen him yesterday, but today his desk had a nameplate with his name on it along with a business card holder completely filled with his business cards.

Sewell was talking to another customer when I got there, so I sat in one of the uncomfortable chairs the bank reserved for people who had to wait to give the bank their money. While I waited, I took the opportunity to observe Sewell in his natural habitat.

His customer was an elderly woman with long white hair that hung nearly to her waist and looked far thicker than mine. Her eyes were bright with amusement as he chatted with her like she was his best friend. He leaned forward in his seat to catch something she said, his interest riveted on her, and when he chuckled in response, the woman actually blushed.

Unlike a lot of people in service positions who had to deal with the elderly, Sewell seemed in no hurry to rush this woman. I sat waiting for twenty minutes while the two of them talked. Sewell occasionally typed something into his computer, and at one point the women took a card of some type out of her purse and showed it to him.

As they neared the end of the conversation, Sewell printed out forms for the woman to sign, and she handed over a wad of cash from her purse that made me lift my eyebrows. She'd either won big at one of the casinos or cleaned out the stash she'd been keeping under her mattress for the last forty years.

Sewell had to walk by me to take the cash to one of the teller windows. He spotted me waiting, and the smile he'd had for the elderly woman dialed up a notch.

"Hello, there!" he said to me. "Great to see you again."

I smiled back. If he didn't remember me, he was doing a good job of faking it. Then again, how many women had tracked him down just to ask if he'd dropped twenty dollars on the street? I'd only done that the day before.

"Are you waiting for me?" he asked.

"If you've got a minute."

My answer pleased him. "For you? I've got two," he said. "Don't go anywhere." And then he was off to the teller line to deposit his customer's cash.

It took another five minutes for him to finish up with the elderly woman. Sewell actually walked her halfway to the glass doors in the wall of floor-to-ceiling windows that opened from the bank into the office building's lobby. She left all smiles with a hint of a blush still staining her cheeks.

"Now, what can I help you with today?" he asked as I sat down in one of his client chairs.

I'd had plenty of time to study the brochures outlining the various accounts the bank offered. "I'm interested in one of your business checking accounts." I wasn't really, but I could fake it.

"Great!"

He went into a short spiel about the types of accounts the

bank offered. He talked with the same charm and enthusiasm I'd seen him display with the elderly lady.

I had to admit, being the focus of all that charisma dialed up to about nine was a little disconcerting. I had to remind myself that this man had been interested in my ex-husband's fiancé and I was only here because I was investigating her death.

A death he didn't seem particularly upset about.

If he'd shed any tears over Melody, I could see no evidence of puffy eyes or the same type of stress I'd noticed in Stacy when I'd met with her at the gym. Did he even know that Melody had died, or would she simply be someone he never heard from again?

After he was done reviewing the accounts his bank offered for small businesses, I settled on a low-cost checking account that I planned to keep open only as long as I absolutely had to. If he was disappointed that I hadn't picked an account with a bunch of bells and whistles and a high monthly service fee, he didn't let it show.

He opened a new screen on his computer and began asking me questions about what type of business I had. I handed him the copy of my private investigator's license that I kept in my wallet.

"You'll find all the information you need on here," I said.

He took the license and peered at it. "Abby Maxon," he said, reading my name printed on the license. "You're really a private investigator?"

"Sounds more glamorous than it is," I said.

"You mean it's not like on television?"

"Most of the time I sit around and wait for people to show up so I can serve them with papers they'd rather not get. Although every now and then..." I lifted an eyebrow and deliberately let the sentence trail off to see whether he'd bite.

He bit.

"You get something interesting?"

I shrugged. "Something like that."

He leaned toward me, like he had with the elderly woman, only now his smile looked conspiratorial.

"Anything you can share?"

I returned the smile. "In this town? The divorce capital of the world? What do you think?"

His expression didn't change but rather seemed to freeze for a split second, almost like he was trying to decide what reaction was most appropriate.

He hadn't paused for a moment when he'd read my last name off my license. Sure, I could have handed him a fake I.D., but I'd wanted to see if he reacted to my last name. Maxon wasn't all that common, but he hadn't tumbled to my connection with Melody through her fiancé's last name.

No. What had tripped him up was the fact that I worked divorce cases, which meant I followed people around trying to catch them in infidelities.

I hadn't been asked to do that often over the course of my career, and most of the time I turned those cases down. Nevada was a no-fault divorce state, which meant neither side needed proof of infidelity to split the sheets. But throw in a prenuptial agreement and bank accounts with more zeros than I'd ever see in my lifetime, and proof of infidelity became a big deal.

I didn't like digging into someone's marital dirty laundry. I wouldn't be doing it now if the stakes weren't so high.

"I bet you see a lot," he said, still smiling that conspiratorial smile, only now it didn't quite reach his eyes.

"Yeah," I said. "I do."

"Well," he said, leaning back in his chair. "Let's get you set up here so you can get back at it."

He didn't chat with me much after that. I'd rattled him, as much as I suspected a man like Justin Sewell could be rattled.

Ed Hastings used to send me books that he thought I

should read just so I'd be prepared for the kind of people I was likely to meet when I was out trying to serve summons and subpoenas on people who didn't want to be found. One of the most disturbing books he'd given me was about the sheer number of sociopaths and psychopaths in the world, most of whom hid in plain sight.

Charming and charismatic, the book had called them. People who didn't mind walking over other people to achieve whatever it was they wanted to achieve. People who faked emotional responses like a pro because they'd spent their entire lives studying and emulating what they thought were normal reactions to any given situation.

I was in danger of releasing my inner Dr. Phil again, but I was pretty sure that Justin Sewell was at least a sociopath.

Was he violent? I had no clue. He could certainly turn his emotions on and off, but not all sociopaths or psychopaths were violent. According to what I'd read, non-violent sociopaths who passed as normal had learned to channel their violent tendencies into some socially acceptable competitive behaviors.

For all I knew, Justin Sewell could have channeled his aggressive tendencies into developing a killer backhand and a murderous serve, charging the net to a first place victory in a local tennis tournament.

But what if Melody had done something that triggered a violent reaction? They'd seemed to part ways after lunch on good terms. Could something have happened that made him snap and kill her just a few hours later?

When Sewell finished setting up my new business account, I wrote a check for the minimum amount required to open the account. He lifted an eyebrow when I handed him the check.

"It'll take me a while to transfer everything over," I said.

He seemed to consider me for another split second. "So why are you really opening this account?" he asked.

I shrugged. "I read the brochure you gave me yesterday. I liked what it said."

His expression told me that he didn't buy it for a minute. "The bank you're with now offers better features for its small business customers than we do."

I decided to play on his vanity. "You're right, but I've yet to be treated as well by anybody there as I've been treated by you. Banks make a big deal about giving personalized service, but what they really want is to sell you everything they possibly can." I gave him a grin I hoped was at least a little flirty. "At least you make me feel good while you do it."

He didn't say anything, but he did seem to be thinking over what I said.

"Tell you what," I said. "Give me the name of your manager, and I'll write a glowing letter about the great customer service you gave me here today. That's got to at least win you brownie points, right?"

He chuckled. "Okay. That I can do. But if you really want to help a guy out, you'll let me tell you about what else the bank can do for your business."

"You get more than brownie points for sales, I'm guessing, than glowing letters extolling your great customer service skills."

He spread his hands in a *what can you do?* gesture. "You can't blame me for trying."

I nodded toward the paperwork I'd just signed. "You've got my name and number. Give me a call sometime, and maybe we can talk about it over a drink."

Now, I had no illusion that I was anywhere near as attractive as any of the women who worked at Right Track Fitness. I certainly wasn't dressed like I had a lot of money. But I could tell that I'd intrigued him, if for no other reason that he didn't know if I knew something about him that he wanted kept secret.

The smile he gave me this time reminded me of a shark's grin. "All right, Abby. I'll keep that in mind."

When he took my check over to the teller line to make the deposit, I sat back in his client chair and wondered if I'd just bitten off more than I could chew.

Ed used to tell stories about how, when he'd been a detective with the Reno Police Department, he used to deliberately push people past their limits to see if he could get them to make a mistake. He had scars from some of the times he'd pushed people too far, including a puckered scar on his right shoulder from a bullet he'd taken when an embezzler thought Ed had backed him into a corner he couldn't get out of. Embezzlement was usually a non-violent crime, and Ed hadn't been ready for the man to come after him with a gun.

I didn't think Sewell would come after me with a gun, but would that change when he discovered my connection to Melody?

I hadn't come to the bank with much of a plan. Mostly I'd wanted to see if he'd had a reaction to Melody's death, and when it didn't look like he had, I'd pushed him. I'd deliberately baited him, and I'd set myself up to get in deeper. I could just imagine telling Kyle that I had a date for drinks with a sociopath.

I glanced toward the front of the bank, trying not to fidget while I waited for Sewell to come back with my deposit receipt so I could leave.

The glass walls at the front of the bank gave me a clear look at the lobby as well as Liberty Street beyond through the floor-to-ceiling windows that made up most of the building's first floor walls. Even in the middle of the afternoon, traffic was heavy on Liberty Street, the cars backed up waiting for the light. In a few more weeks, a lot of that traffic would be Harley Davidson motorcycles when Street Vibrations rolled into town.

One of the secretaries in Ryan's office building had told me once that the heavy rumbling of so many motorcycle engines echoing off the smooth glass and steel of the high-rises downtown made it almost impossible to concentrate on her work.

I could just imagine the noise. My office was downtown too, but in an old converted house a few blocks west of Virginia Street, the main drag through town where the Harleys cruised. Still, whenever a major event like Street Vibrations hit town, I was thankful that most of the time my work took me away from the office.

The light must have changed on Liberty because the cars started moving again. In the gaps between the cars, I could see another bank across the street and the parking lot next door.

A white SUV was parked in the lot.

A white SUV with tinted windows.

I couldn't make out the license plate on the SUV from where I was sitting, and I couldn't very well just get up and walk away before Sewell had a chance to give me the paperwork for my new checking account.

I made myself turn back toward Sewell's desk. I pulled my cell phone out of my purse just to give myself something else to look at so I wouldn't be tempted to turn around and stare at the SUV again.

If that was Richards in the SUV, what the hell was he doing here? Was he watching Sewell now? Why? Because he thought Sewell had something to do with what happened to Melody?

An ugly thought crept in. Richards had taken a picture of me yesterday while I was in line to get gas. He knew what my car looked like, what my license plate number was.

What if he was following me?

But why? Did he suspect I had something to do with Melody's death, just like Archulette and Squires did? Richards was suspended. He wouldn't be involved in that investigation.

I almost jumped out of my seat when Sewell came up behind me and handed me the deposit receipt.

"Thanks," I said, trying to recover with a grin that probably looked as shaky as I felt.

He knew he'd startled me. I could see the enjoyment in his eyes even though he was giving me his best professional, personal banker smile.

"You're all set," he said. He gathered all the paperwork together for my new account and tucked it carefully inside a portfolio, making sure to tuck one of his business cards inside. "Just in case you lost my card from yesterday, now you know how to reach me."

"And you know how to reach me," I said. "If you ever want that drink."

His eyes locked with mine for just a moment, and I swore I caught a glimpse the dangerous man who lurked beneath Sewell's civilized mask. "Be careful, Abby Maxon," he said. "I might be more than you can handle."

I didn't doubt that for a minute.

Playing with fire, Kyle had said. He'd been referring to Richards, but I had a feeling Sewell was really the guy I had to watch out for.

## 22

I'd left my car in the parking garage attached to the bank building, safely tucked into one of the spaces earmarked for the bank's customers.

A sign at the front of the space warned that parking was limited to twenty minutes. I'd been inside the bank for over an hour. Did the bank give out parking tickets?

I certainly hoped not. I'd just put money I couldn't afford to tie up into an account I couldn't close for a month without incurring a penalty. At least I had a temporary debit card for cash withdrawals if I needed the money in a pinch. I just didn't want to use that money to pay for a parking ticket, especially since I wasn't spending my day working for a paying client.

The security guard in the building's lobby raised his eyebrows as I walked past him on the way to my car. I smiled at him, and he gave me a nod and touched his cap in a quick salute. He thought I'd scored a date. Maybe I had, but it wasn't the kind of date the guard assumed it would be.

Kyle was not going to be happy with me. I should probably give him a call. I dug my phone out of my purse again and looked at the display as I made my way from the building into the attached parking garage. No bars on my phone. The parking garage had five upper levels. All that concrete must be interfering with cell phone reception. I'd have to wait to call Kyle until I was on the road.

Distracted by the phone and the conversation I'd just had with Sewell, I didn't realize I wasn't alone until it was too late.

Lewis Richards was leaning against the driver's side of my car, muscular arms crossed over his chest, waiting for me.

This time I did jump.

Richards wasn't smiling, and the look in his eyes was no less dangerous than Sewell's.

"Abby Maxon," he said. "We need to talk."

His voice was cold, which was at odds with his casual posture.

He reminded me of a cat pretending to sleep when all the while she was watching a mouse creep ever so slowly closer through the grass, content to bide her time until the mouse got within striking distance. I'd watched the cat that had walked along my backyard fence that morning do exactly that, go from apparent sleep to pouncing on a mouse I hadn't even known was in my lawn.

I had no intention of being Lewis Richards' mouse.

I gestured with the phone I still held in my hand. "Give me a call," I said. "Anytime. I'm in the book, or you can Google me. I have a website."

It was a smartass response and I knew it. Probably not the wisest choice of words I'd ever made considering the only thing I had to defend myself with was the cell phone I held in my hand and a can of pepper spray in my pursue. Oh, and the car keys that were still shoved in the pocket of my jeans. If Richards decided to get physical, I doubted I could reach the pepper spray or keys fast enough to do me any good.

Richards might have been undercover for years, but he still had the intimidating cop stare down pat.

Unfortunately for him, I'd started to recover from my initial surprise. I didn't care about the intimidating stare or the fact that he was taller than I was and outweighed me by at least fifty pounds of solid muscle, and that he might have had something to do with Melody's death. He was standing between me and my car, and he expected me to do what he wanted just because he said so. Not going to happen.

"I have an appointment, and you're making me late," I said.

I knew my stare couldn't intimidate worth a damn, but I glared at him anyway.

We must have looked strange to anyone driving by looking for a parking space or gazing out at the parking garage from inside the glass-enclosed walkway that led to the elevators to the upper levels of the garage. Richards still leaned against my car, the pose casual except for the crossed arms, and I probably looked like a little rat terrier straining on her leash.

If Richards wasn't careful, I'd be launching into another rant like the one I'd given Stacy earlier in the day.

Richards finally shifted position. He didn't step away from the car as much as straighten his posture so that he was no longer leaning on my car. He broke eye contact to glance at my phone. Probably making sure I hadn't speed-dialed 9-1-1.

"I need to talk to you," he said. His voice had lost its cold edge and instead had an urgency that hadn't been there before. "You're making a mistake. I don't want it to cost you."

"Cost me what?"

"What you're trying to protect."

I didn't trust Richards as far as I could throw him. Considering I probably couldn't even pick him up, that wasn't very far.

I still didn't know if he'd followed me here or if he'd decided to start following Sewell. I didn't know why he'd been arguing with Melody yesterday, although given the intensity of his first conversation with me, I was starting to think that what I'd seen had been a normal conversation where Richards was concerned. And I definitely had no clue how he could know anything about me other than what was public information.

On the other hand, I had nothing concrete on Sewell or Richards or anything to do with Melody's murder that I could take to the police that would make them turn their search for her killer away from Ryan. I didn't even know if he was still just a person of interest or whether he'd been upgraded to a suspect. I hoped that Norton would call me if Ryan had been arrested, even if it was just to give me a heads-up so that I could prepare Samantha before she heard it on the news, or worse yet, from one of her friends.

I certainly hadn't figured out how to get the kind of information I needed on Richards, the kind of information that Kyle wouldn't be able to get from his chatty friends on the force. Stacy had only given me background, and from what she'd told me, Richards had seemed like the possessive type.

Might as well plow ahead and see what I could get. The best way I knew how to do that was to knock him as off balance as he'd meant to knock me by waiting for me where I least expected to see him.

"Did you kill her?" I asked.

He rocked back a little, his body rigid. I don't think he took a breath for nearly half a minute. The only thing that looked alive about him were his eyes. I had a hard time looking at the pain reflected there.

"Is that what you think?" he finally asked, the question almost inaudible over the sound of traffic on the street and a car horn echoing off the walls of the garage.

"I think you're dangerous when you want to be. I think you were following her yesterday, and you were in the middle of an argument when I saw the both of you at the gym. I think you might have been obsessed with her, and you didn't like the fact that she had lunch with another man."

He lifted an eyebrow and opened his mouth, but I wasn't done yet.

"I think you took my picture with your cell phone yesterday and maybe you've been following me, although I didn't spot your car until about ten minutes ago. I think the police took the convenient, easy way out when they interviewed me trying to dig up dirt on Ryan's relationship with her when they could have had at least two easier suspects if they'd only widened the investigation a little further, but you'd know what kind of conclusions cops would jump to, wouldn't you? But you know what I think most of all? I think maybe someone set up Ryan to be a convenient patsy."

I hadn't consciously considered that last part, but it had flowed out of me in a logical chain and I went with it.

What if someone *had* been setting Ryan up? With the flowers and the pictures and the phone calls, knowing what conclusions a lawyer might draw from the evidence at hand?

"I didn't kill her." Richards took a deep breath and glanced around the garage as if to check to see if anyone was listening. Apparently satisfied no one was close enough to hear, he looked back at me. "She was my informant," he said.

Now it was my turn to be shocked. That was the last thing I'd expected to hear.

"You're suspended," I said. "How could she..."

He was staring over my shoulder. I turned my head to see the security guard watching us from inside the glassed-in walkway. Several other people were waiting for the elevator. They couldn't hear us, but they sure could see us.

"We can't talk here," Richards said. "Let's go for a ride."

"If you think I'm getting—"

"Look, I'm still a cop," he said, interrupting me. "I was never suspended. That was just a cover story. Make you feel any better?"

Not really, but I agreed that we couldn't keep talking here.

We were attracting too much attention as it was. If Sewell left on a break, or even left to go get something out of his car, I didn't want him to see me talking to Richards. I had a feeling this wasn't going to be the kind of conversation either of us wanted overheard, so that ruled out a bar or a restaurant. At least I knew my car was safe.

I dug my car keys out of my pocket and thumbed the fob, unlocking the doors. "Are you armed?" I asked him.

He shook his head. "I'm not supposed to be a cop anymore, remember?"

"Well, I've got a can of pepper spray in my purse, which I'm going to put on the seat right next to me." I pointed at the passenger side of my car. "The door's unlocked."

I dug the pepper spray out of my purse while he walked around the front of my car. I got in the driver's seat, tempted for a moment to lock the doors and just leave. Only the possibility of Ryan's arrest for murder made me stay.

Richards opened the passenger door and leaned in. "You don't trust me one bit, do you?" he asked.

I lifted the pepper spray in response. It hadn't escaped me that Melody had been killed in her own car.

"I don't blame you," he said as he slid in the passenger seat and buckled himself in. "I don't blame you at all."

# 23

I've put a lot of miles on my car. Reno isn't the biggest place in the world, and I'm sure other people have longer commutes, but Nevada is a big state with a whole lot of nothing in between the towns that dot the desert.

I've served subpoenas in Silver Springs and Stagecoach and Gerlach, and once I tracked a witness down on the Pyramid Lake Paiute reservation. When Samantha was in elementary school, she played soccer three afternoons a week after school, and I went to every game I could. So far we'd made seven trips to Nevada City and back just so Samantha could spent time with Jonathan.

I never minded driving. I enjoyed Samantha's company when she was with me, and when I was alone, I enjoyed listening to audiobooks. The stories made the time in the car fly by, but I never got so involved in the plot that I lost track of where I was driving and why.

Driving around town with no destination in mind with a potentially dangerous man in my passenger seat was not an enjoyable experience. It didn't matter that he was a cop. Cops could be killers just like anyone else.

I left the bank building and headed west on California. My plan was to get on McCarran and just keep driving so that I wouldn't get distracted by downtown traffic.

McCarran ran in a continuous loop through Reno and Sparks. The original intent of the road was to ring around the outside of both cities, providing residents with an alternative to the two freeways through town—I-80 ran east and west and 395 north and south—that were becoming increasingly clogged with traffic. By the time all the sections of McCarran were completed, both cities had grown beyond the outer edge of the McCarran loop.

These days McCarran was just another major thoroughfare dotted with traffic lights in the congested areas but boasting a higher speed limit than most city streets. On the plus side for me, the road had an almost continual flow of traffic, not to mention a good percentage of patrol cars on the lookout for speeders.

Even though Richards had said we needed to talk, he didn't say anything until we'd passed the cafe on California where Melody had had lunch the day before. I almost expected to see the same older guy sitting at a table out front, reading something on his tablet, but lunch time was long over and the outside tables were empty.

"I didn't set your ex up," Richards said. "Archulette and Squires are good detectives, but they don't think outside the box, and the box says look to the spouse or significant other whenever someone gets killed after a domestic disturbance."

Domestic disturbance. He must be referring to the scene Melody threw at Ryan's office after I left the gym.

"How much do you know about the investigation?" I asked. "Is Ryan going to be charged?"

"Not much. Everybody in the department except my captain thinks I've been suspended, so I'm the black sheep." He looked down at his hands. "It wasn't much of a stretch. I can be

a pain in the ass. So no, I don't know if they're going to recom-
mend that your ex be charged, or if they're investigating any
other leads."

Kyle had described Richards as a little prick, but now that
I'd had a chance to observe him up close and listen to him talk,
he struck me more as a punk kid grown up.

He wasn't that much taller than I was, although he was
bulkier and more solid than he first appeared. He was wearing
a plain white tank top that showed off the definition of the
muscles in his shoulders and chest, but his olive skin bore faint
scars from adolescent skin problems and other, less innocent,
damage.

With his dirty blond hair and dark eyes, put him in a watch
cap or a hoodie, and he'd be the guy other people would be
frightened of in a dark alley. I could see why he'd been chosen
for undercover drug work. Thirty pounds skinnier, hair a little
longer and unkempt, and he'd have no trouble passing for a
drug-using gang banger.

"You said I was making a mistake that would cost me," I said
as we passed the turnoff to Keystone Avenue. "What mistake?"

"Pushing Justin Sewell."

"What makes you think I'm pushing him?"

Richards considered me for a moment. "How much do you
know about Sewell?"

So we were going to play "you show me yours and I'll show
you mine." Okay, I'd bite. After all, I'd let him in my car.

"He was born in Boca Raton," I said. "He did work for a
charity in Boca called the Widows and Orphans of Southern
Florida. It's on his LinkedIn profile, buried among all the local
charities he volunteers for because his bank requires it. The
Widows and Orphans of Southern Florida owns a Florida LLC
that, several times removed, owns a piece of a resort called the
Boca Beach Club, which is owned by a guy named Antonio
Gordino. A few years back, Gordino managed to get out from

under federal racketeering and money laundering charges. Sewell lives above his means for a personal banker, but not so much above his means that he'd attract the wrong kind of attention. I can't prove it, but I think he's getting regular money from the charity—call him a consultant or a financial advisor or whatever—but what he's really doing is laundering mo—"

"Jesus," Richards said, interrupting me. "How the fuck did you find all that out?"

"Private investigator," I said. "Seriously motivated private investigator." I didn't tell him that I'd stumbled on most of this by accident. I figured it couldn't hurt if he thought I was just that good.

"I don't think I want to know what you've found out about me."

It hadn't been nearly as much as I'd discovered about Sewell, so I kept my mouth shut. Instead I gave him a sideways glance.

"Okay," he said. "I guess it's my turn."

"That would be nice."

He rubbed a hand over his mouth. "I tumbled onto Sewell by accident, back when everybody thought I was just another burned-out undercover cop who got too deep into the lifestyle. Sewell was pushing prescription drugs—oxy, stuff like that—and I was trying to get a handle on his supplier."

I'd been given a prescription for oxycontin in December when I'd dislocated my shoulder. I'd taken exactly one pill, and it had made me so sick that it was easier to just deal with the pain with over-the-counter pain meds. I'd taken the rest of the pills back to the pharmacy so they could dispose of them.

When I'd mentioned that to Kyle on our first date, he'd told me oxy was a high-demand drug on the streets, and it was also one of the kinds of pills kids stole from their parents' medicine cabinets to get high. I remembered being both appalled at the idea and annoyed that anyone would think Samantha or her friends would do such a thing. Now I wasn't so sure about Maddie.

"Getting in good with a guy like Sewell's tricky," Richards said. "I meant it when I said you were making a mistake going after him. I didn't think you knew what you were stumbling into. Guys like Sewell eat nice, good-looking women for lunch. But you know a lot more than I thought, and you're still going after him."

"Does that mean you no longer think I'm nice?"

"I think you're fucking nuts, but you've got balls. Either that or you've still got a thing for your ex. Mine would just as soon shoot me herself."

"Gloria," I said.

He shot me a sideways glance. "What the hell don't you know?"

I slowed down for a red light on Hunter Lake Drive. The air conditioning in my car was doing its best against the late afternoon heat, but I still felt sweat trickle down my back between my shoulder blades. I considered turning up the fan to high, but the noise would discourage conversation, and I wanted Richards to keep talking.

A young woman on a bicycle pulled to a stop at the light, crowding close to the passenger side of the car in front of me. She was dressed in black bicycle shorts, a bright orange top with black and yellow highlights, and had a plain white helmet on her head. Her bare arms were deeply tanned, and her legs were lean and muscular, the tendons standing out in sharp relief.

I wondered how much of her life was spent on her bike, riding around town at a slow pace or racing up and down the hilly parts of McCarran just for the joy of experiencing the world rushing by without being enclosed in a car. Would she change anything about her life if she knew it might end today?

Melody hadn't known that her life would end yesterday.

She'd been just another young woman going about her day without a clue how precious every remaining second was.

Apparently Richards' question hadn't been rhetorical. He was waiting for an answer.

"I don't know why Melody was murdered," I said. "I don't know who killed her and torched the car. I don't know what message that was supposed to send. I don't know who's setting Ryan up and dragging me along for the ride. Is that enough for you? It's more than enough for me."

He sat quiet. He didn't look like I'd pissed him off, which was good because I was clearly still having trouble controlling my own anger.

My instinct was to apologize for the outburst. I didn't, and not only because I didn't know if Richards had anything to do with her death. I didn't apologize because no one else seemed angry that her life had been snuffed out. Even Stacy, who'd been Melody's best friend, was still stuck in her grief, as I knew Ryan must be.

I had been the furthest thing possible from a friend to Melody. That distance let me move through the grief faster, but it was beginning to look like I wouldn't move past anger until I found out who'd really killed her.

"I didn't kill her," Richards finally said.

"Did you get her killed? Whatever she was doing for you?"

He was staring out the front windshield. The late afternoon sun was directly in his face. I'd had to lower the visor so I could see well enough to drive, but he hadn't moved his. When he started talking, he didn't answer me directly.

"Sewell was a shrewd customer. Most guys like him, they think they're slick enough they'll never get caught, so they don't plan ahead. Sewell, he was different. He tested the variables, calculated the odds, and he did it in a split second, so fast most people wouldn't notice."

I wondered if that's what Sewell had been doing when he'd

seemed to check out for a split second during our conversation after I'd implied I investigated illicit affairs. Calculating the best response given all the possible outcomes.

"I had a few meets with him, bought some pills off him, always trolling to see if I could get a bead on his supplier," Richards said. "Just about the time I'm ready to give up and tell my handler we've got enough on Sewell to arrest his ass, he tells me he just got back from a vacation and guess who he ran into? My ex."

"Gloria," I said as I made the missing connection between Sewell and Richards.

"Yeah. I guess you know who she works for."

I hadn't known she was still working for Gordino, but I did now.

"Gordo's some far-flung relative of hers," Richards said. "Back when we were married, I wasn't a cop yet. She was out here working at one of the casinos, learning the business, she said. I was dealing twenty-one, trying to figure out what I wanted to do with my life. She never planned to stay out here. I thought I could change her mind, she thought she could convince me to go with her when she went back to Boca. I fucking hate snakes, and anybody who hates snakes shouldn't live in Florida. I said no and meant it, and that was the end of us."

He was telling me far more than he had to, but I supposed it was his way of backing into an answer he didn't want to give.

"How did Sewell put it together?" I asked. "That you were her ex. Don't you have a cover name?"

"That's the beauty of it. There's this thing in twenty-one called Five Card Charlie. This place I worked, I was one of the youngest dealers there, and most of the rest of them were women. Everybody gave me shit, started calling me Charlie. The name stuck. I had to put Lewis on the marriage license, but when Gloria met me, everybody called me Charlie, so she did too. That's the name I go by now, Charlie Richards."

Which explained why I hadn't found a current credit history for Lewis Richards. If I was a betting woman, which I'm not, I would bet that almost everything he did these days was on a cash basis.

We'd reached McCarran. The woman on the bicycle was far behind us. I put on the signal and got in the left-hand turn lane to go south on McCarran, the opposite way I'd gone the day before when I took this route to Melody's gym. Driving by the café on California had been tough enough.

If Richards noticed we weren't going by the gym, he didn't say. Instead he continued his part of our little mutual show and tell.

"When Sewell got back from his little vacation and told me he met my ex, I got curious. I hadn't thought about Gloria in years. I looked her up, found out who she's working for. Suddenly my little fish starts to look like somebody who can lead me to something big. Since I couldn't get a handle on where he was getting the meds he was dealing, I figured, why not? I reported in through my handler, and the next thing I know, I'm being hauled in by the Feds who want to know what my connections are to the Gordino family. I thought I was fucked."

"Instead you found yourself with a new assignment," I said.

"They came up with the cover story that I'd been suspended for using the products I was trying to get off the street."

The way Richards said it, I could tell that part of the cover story didn't sit well with him.

"They cut me off from everybody but my captain. I think they got burned by somebody on the inside the last time around, somebody who made their case against Gordino disappear. They made it pretty clear I was on my own—not even my handler could know what I was really doing—and they'd cut me loose and let me fry if I fucked up."

I could just imagine how it all must have gone down. The Feds had been embarrassed by Gordino all those years ago. Here was a local undercover cop who already had a connection with someone who might be on Gordino's payroll. If he screwed up, he wasn't one of theirs, so they wouldn't have to make an uncomfortable "no comment" to the press about why they let Gordino skate. Again.

The one thing he hadn't told me was how Melody figured in all this. All he'd said was that she'd been his informant, but he already had a connection with Sewell. What did he need her for?

"I don't understand what all this had to do with Melody," I said.

"She was his girlfriend," Richards said.

# 24

-------

Girlfriend? Melody was Justin Sewell's *girlfriend?*

If I hadn't spent years driving with one eye on the road and the other eye imagining the world of the audiobook I was listening to, I probably would have smashed the car against one of the concrete barriers on the far side of the shoulder meant to prevent distracted drivers from sailing off the road and landing on top of one of the million-dollar Caughlin Park houses that crowded against McCarran.

I suddenly understood with perfect clarity the meaning behind three initials Samantha and her friends seemed to use all the time—*WTF.*

"Ryan proposed to Melody on Valentine's Day," I said to Richards. "She said yes."

Even though Ryan didn't tell us right away, I remembered the date pretty damn clearly. I could still hear the happiness in his voice when he told me. Why wouldn't he be happy? He'd been in love.

"How could she be engaged to Ryan and still be Justin Sewell's girlfriend? How is that possible?"

The question was rhetorical. I knew things like that happened all the time. Richards answered me anyway.

"She was a party girl," he said. "I met her through Sewell. She was one of his customers."

He didn't mean the bank, although that might have been where she'd met him. No, Richards meant that Melody bought drugs from Sewell.

I thought back to the night when Ryan had been late picking up Samantha because he had to wait for Melody, and she'd been late. I'd assumed she was drunk, that she'd been out drinking with friends and either lost track of or didn't care about the time. About the fact that she'd kept Ryan and Samantha waiting.

Had she been drunk that night? Or had she been stoned instead? Did Ryan even know that she took drugs?

Did he know about any of it?

Did Stacy? She'd been so vehement that Melody had never cheated on Ryan, but suddenly all the pictures on Melody's Facebook wall, the ones without Ryan in them, made sense.

Everything made sense. The single red roses. The phone calls to the house by the man who'd hang up whenever Ryan answered the phone. The photographs of Melody. She didn't have a stalker. She'd been having an affair.

"I couldn't get close enough to Sewell," Richards said. "He didn't trust me. I was just some street dealer he needed so he could unload his stuff. The feds were pressuring me. I had to figure out a way to get what I needed. I spotted the two of them together. I tailed her, figured out where she worked, what she did."

"And you hired her as your personal trainer," I said.

"Yeah." He looked down at his hands again as he flexed them, the muscles in his arms bunching beneath his skin. "She was damn good at it, too. That was her problem. She thought she was good at everything."

"Even being a spy?"

"Something like that."

"So," I said, "let me get this straight. You recruited Melody to get information for you that would tie Sewell to some illegal activity that involved Gordino. How did you manage to do that?"

"She had a pretty cushy life going with your ex. She didn't want to lose that."

He'd blackmailed her. Threatened to take all the information he had on her to Ryan if she didn't do what he wanted.

"You bastard," I said.

My voice was shaking. Hell, I was wound so tight my entire body was shaking.

"I am that," he said.

We drove more than a mile in silence. We passed an exclusive golf course on the far side of Caughlin Park. The professional office buildings clustered around Plumas and Lakeside. The sprawling, green-roofed medical complex near Talbot.

When we stopped at the lights near Meadowood Mall, I thought about turning onto Virginia Street and heading downtown so I could take Richards back to his car.

Hell, I thought about kicking him to the curb. Let him take the bus. I didn't want to be around him for one more minute, but I had to know.

"Who killed her?" I asked.

He scrubbed at his face with his hands. "I wish to hell I knew."

"One of Gordino's people?"

"I don't know."

"Sewell?"

"I don't fucking know!"

He glared at me, his face flushed with more than just anger, but I wasn't about to let him off the hook.

"You were arguing with her at the gym when I showed up yesterday," I said. "What was that about?"

For a minute I thought he wasn't going to tell me. The idea of kicking him out of my car was starting to sound better and better.

"She'd started fucking up," he eventually said. "Getting careless. Almost like she wanted to get caught, have some big blow up with your ex or something. I had a tracker on her car, so I followed her, trying to watch out for her, then she goes and has lunch with the guy at that place on California. So we got in an argument about it, then she shows me this key, like it's a big prize. She says it's the key to Sewell's place."

"He gave her a key?" I could see Sewell sleeping with someone like Melody, but I couldn't see him giving anyone a key.

"You know that spy shop in midtown? She bought a kit there, this thing to make duplicate keys. I didn't even know about it until she showed me the key, all proud of herself. She was in the middle of telling me how she planned to go to his apartment to see what she could find while he was at work, then you showed up, and she lost her shit a whole different way."

Now I understood why. She'd thought Ryan had me following her to find out if she was screwing around on him, which she was.

I wondered if the argument she'd had with Ryan at his office had convinced her he'd thought she only had a stalker, not a secret boyfriend.

"To her, it was all a game," Richards said. "She always got her way with men. She didn't want to screw things up with Ryan. Your ex, he's making good money, and I guess she liked the lifestyle. He didn't care if she went out with her girlfriends, but with Sewell it was something different."

Of course, it was. Sewell was a bad boy, something Ryan

had never been. He'd been a jock, but he'd been a smart, motivated jock. He worked hard, played by the rules for the most part, and he was a good dad to Samantha.

If Melody had a deep, dark fascination with bad boys, life with Ryan would have become boring, no matter how much money he made or how many parties she went to without him.

"Sewell knew all about Ryan and told her he didn't care. He would have cared if he'd found out about the rest, but I couldn't make her understand she had to be careful," Richards said. "That's what I need you to understand. Why I told you all this. You didn't start out a cop. You have no idea how dangerous a guy like Sewell can be. You need to back off before he figures out who you are. That you were connected to Melody."

A sliver of ice ran down my spine.

Sewell knew who I was and what I did.

My private investigator's license only had my office address, same with the check I'd written to open my bright, shiny new account, but Maxon wasn't a common name. If Sewell was motivated enough, he could find my home address in any number of databases, from the Assessor's Office right down to the Recorder's Office. People called it "public information" for a reason, and a banker like Sewell would know exactly how to find it.

"I appreciate the heads up," I said. "But it's a little late for that."

## 25

Instead of driving the entire McCarran loop, I doubled back to Plumas and headed toward downtown.

I needed to get in touch with Kyle, and I didn't want to do that with Richards in the car. I needed to call Samantha and make sure she was all right. I'd left her alone for too long, especially on a day like today.

Most of all I needed to call Norton so I could tell him what I'd learned from Richards, see if he could use any of that information to get Archulette and Squires to back off Ryan. I didn't care if it blew Richards' undercover operation sky high. I didn't owe him anything. His little undercover operation had already done too much damage.

I thought Richards would read me the riot act once he realized how much Sewell knew about me. He didn't. He also didn't tell me how stupid I'd been. He just sat in the passenger seat, staring out the windshield, probably thinking about how he was going to salvage what was left of his investigation.

I figured I had about another fifteen minutes in the car with Richards before I dropped him off. I didn't care if he wanted to ride in silence. I intended to put the time to good use. There was a lot about the case I still didn't know.

"I still don't understand why you needed Melody," I said. "Can't you just trace the money? Follow a paper trail?"

Richards seemed to rouse himself from somewhere far away. He gave me a quick glance, and I was surprised to see a sadness in his eyes that didn't show in his expression. I remembered that Stacy said Melody had flirted with Richards as well, selling her sex appeal. Had Richards fallen for his informant?

"Paper trail," he said. "If only it was that simple. Guys who work for someone like Gordo, they keep two sets of books. One set's squeaky clean, kept in an obvious place, like a program on Sewell's laptop, just in case someone comes calling with a search warrant. That's all we'd find, a nice, neat set of numbers that tracks all of Sewell's income from his bank job and the money he gets from the charity and about a dozen other businesses for consulting work. He even reports all that income on his taxes. He's a smart guy. He doesn't want to get nabbed for tax evasion."

He shifted in his seat, tugging at the seatbelt where it rubbed against his collarbone. I noticed that he'd started lumping himself in with the Feds as he talked. I wondered if he'd been promised a permanent job with the F.B.I. if he did well on this case.

"Then there's the other set of books," Richards said. "The set where he keeps track of the amount of money that comes in and what he does with it. He's got to keep track of every penny because someone like Gordino, he can smell when someone's skimming off the top, and Sewell might have to prove someday that he was a good little soldier."

"So you wanted Melody to find the second set of books."

"If she could. Mostly I wanted her to get Sewell to live beyond his means. Way beyond his means. If he was doing what the feds thought he was doing for Gordino—"

"Laundering money," I said.

"Yeah. Running it through the bank into accounts for dummy companies, making enough small deposits to enough different accounts so that nobody would notice. A guy like that, with access to all that money, he starts to think he's smarter than the boss, and maybe the big guy won't notice if a couple hundred here or there goes missing."

"One thing I don't understand is where he got all this money," I said. It wasn't like someone could just send him a check in the mail. Could they?

"Lots of different ways," Richards said. "Say you've got a lot of cash you need to make look legit. You've got a guy you can trust, so you give him some of it. He goes into a casino and buys a bunch of chips with dirty money. Not enough to put him on the casino's radar. He sits down at a table, plays for a while—maybe he wins, maybe he loses, but never enough to draw attention from the pit boss—then he goes and cashes out all his chips. Now the cash in his pocket is gambling winnings, no longer dirty money."

"Is that what Sewell was doing?"

"We think so. At least that was part of it. Melody told me she'd met him in a casino bar. He'd been throwing around money, bought her and her girlfriends a few rounds. Said he'd won big at the tables."

The pictures I'd seen on her Facebook wall. Had that been the night she'd met Sewell?

"We also think he's been getting cashier's checks in the mail," Richards said. "He deposits them into accounts for the dummy corporations. At the other end, somebody takes dirty money into a bank, buys cashier's checks or money orders payable to one of the companies Sewell set up. Probably nothing over a few thousand dollars, nothing that would raise eyebrows. Same thing on this end. Sewell's an officer or member of more than a dozen companies registered in Nevada.

Spend a couple hundred bucks a year in fees to the state, and bam—he's got himself a new business. It doesn't matter that all the business does is receive and disburse money. Some to Sewell, some to other consultants or project managers who dummy up development plans for projects that never happen, who hire work done by other companies owned by—"

"Gordino," I said.

"Or owned by other companies he owns."

I'd spent a lot of time running down all the companies that owned Breakers, but I'd never searched through corporate records in Nevada to see if Sewell owned any companies here. I knew he worked at a bank. I hadn't thought far enough outside the box to check to see if he was involved in any other businesses. So much for congratulating myself on my stellar detective skills.

"The companies issue fake invoices to account for the money they receive," Richards said. "On the surface, it's business as usual, nothing illegal."

Sewell was in the perfect position within the bank to handle all the money. He brought deposits to the tellers all the time. He was charming and charismatic. He probably flirted with the single tellers and charmed the married ones, and I'd almost bet he never took his deposits to a male teller unless he had to.

No one ever caught on that the deposits weren't for the customer whose account he'd just opened. And he never stayed in one branch long enough for anyone to notice a pattern.

"Where he could get himself in trouble is with the cash," Richards said. "Large sums of cash coming in at irregular intervals is hard to keep track of, especially when he's spreading it out over lots of different companies. The deposits all have to be under ten grand, or paperwork gets filed with the government. If Melody started making demands, hinting around that she wanted something special, say a ring to outdo the one Ryan gave her, Sewell might dip into that cash to keep her happy. Once that happened, we have people at the other end who can plant a rumor that the numbers aren't adding up at Sewell's end. He gets nervous, and that's when we'd turn up the heat."

I gave him a long sideways glance. "This whole operation is to get Sewell to flip."

"Make no mistake, we wouldn't mind busting him, but we're really after his bosses. The ultimate prize would be Gordino, but it's like a game of dominos. Get Sewell to flip on the guys who decide how much money comes his way and from what source, and maybe one of them will flip on a guy higher up."

"And along the way, people get hurt. People get killed. I suppose they're just collateral damage, right?"

His mouth thinned into a tight line, and those dark eyes went flat. I'd hurt him, but he wasn't going to let me see it.

"You know this whole thing is seriously screwed up, right?" I asked. "It's like a high-stakes game of chess. Only this isn't a game. You're screwing with innocent people's lives."

"Melody wasn't innocent."

"And so what if she wasn't? Did you tell her she might die? She was stupid and selfish and she cheated on a man who loved her, but last time I checked, those weren't death penalty offenses."

He didn't say anything.

We were nearing California Avenue. He told me to drop him at the corner of Liberty and Sierra, only a block away.

Traffic was starting to get heavy as office workers in the surrounding buildings started to make their way home for the night. Richards' white SUV sat off by itself now in the almost empty parking lot. I guessed that bank must have closed at four. Only the drive thru windows were still busy.

I'd been gone longer than I thought. I'd have to talk to Norton while I drove home to check on Samantha. I hoped he didn't mind being on speaker phone.

I pulled into a loading zone near the corner where Richards wanted me to drop him off. Before he got out of the car, I asked him if it was all worth it.

He gave me a long look. "I have to believe the answer's yes," he said. "Most days? I just don't know."

He was already across the street by the time I got a break in traffic and made the turn onto Liberty. It would be the quickest way home, even if it did put my car on display if Sewell happened to be looking out the front of the bank.

Would he still be there? It occurred to me that I had no clue what hours he worked. Sewell's bank stayed open until five. Just because he'd gone back to work after his lunch with Melody didn't mean he worked until the bank closed. What was the old joke about banker's hours? If he ended his day at four, he could be anywhere.

Like on his way to my house.

Crap.

I fished my cell phone out of purse while I was stopped in traffic. I had just speed-dialed my house when I heard a dull *whump* from somewhere behind me, and then the sound of people screaming.

I saw a cloud of black smoke in my rearview mirror. Even as I twisted around in my seat, some part of me knew where the smoke was coming from.

Richards' white SUV was on fire.

## 26

Instead of heading toward home, I decided to make a quick circle around the block. Well, as quick as I could manage with downtown traffic and one-way streets.

Richards had been in his car when it caught fire, I had no doubt about that. Unlike when a car explodes in the movies or on TV, there'd been no huge fireball rising into the sky. No, this had been a quick, contained explosion designed to kill only one man, and I needed to take a look. Not to make sure that it had been Richards' car that had gone up in flames.

I wanted to see if Sewell was watching the car burn.

"Hello?"

Samantha's voice came over the speaker in my phone. In my shock at the explosion, I'd forgotten I'd called her.

"Hi, honey," I said. "I just wanted to check in, see how you're doing."

I tried to keep my voice calm. I must have failed miserably.

"What's wrong, Mom?"

I took a deep breath. "It's been a long, very weird day."

A black Porsche cut in front of me, and I had to slam on the brakes. I felt like honking the horn at the driver, but that wouldn't get me where I was going any faster.

"Dad never called back," Samantha said. "I didn't even talk to Jonathan long, just in case he called me on my cell." She paused, and I could almost see her biting her lower lip. She used to bite her nails when she was younger. Now her lower lip took the abuse when she was worried. "Do you think he's okay?"

Any assurances I could have given her would have rung false. "No, I don't think he's okay, but I think he will be. We just have to give him time."

I'd managed to make it about halfway through the loop of downtown streets I needed to take to make my circle. My plan was to drive past the courthouses and take the one-way street that would bring me next to the parking lot where Richards had parked his SUV.

I'd have to move fast. I could hear sirens echoing off the downtown high rises. Rush hour traffic would slow down response teams, but as soon as the cops arrived, they'd cordon off the area, and I'd lose chance to get a look at the crowd.

I took the street in front of the courthouses faster than I should have, and I had to slam on the brakes to let two uniformed deputies cross the street in front of me. They were running toward the fire, talking on their radios as they ran. One of them had a hand on his holstered sidearm.

I wasn't surprised. A few years ago one of the judges had been shot while he was in his office. The bullet had been fired from a high-powered rifle in a parking garage two blocks away.

As soon as I could, I made the turn onto the one-way street. I took the corner too fast, and the pepper spray I still had on the seat next to my leg rolled off onto the floor. A car horn blared behind me.

"Mom? What was that?"

"Crazy driver," I said, not mentioning that the crazy driver was me. I didn't drive like that when I had Samantha in the car. She'd be getting her own driver's license soon, and I wanted to set a good example.

It shouldn't have taken me long to get to the parking lot. It was only one long city block away from where I'd turned onto the one-way street, but traffic was already snarled as drivers slowed to a crawl to gawk at the burning car. Well, at least the traffic jam would give me a chance to take a good long look at the crowd.

And there was a crowd. Most of the people who'd stopped to watch the car burn were across the street in front of the bank building where Sewell worked. The people on my side of the street were actually giving the parking lot a wide berth. Like me, they'd probably watched too many movies where burning cars turned into gigantic fireballs.

Driving by, even slowly, didn't give me as good a look at the crowd as I wanted. My camera had a video function. I could have used it to take a video of the crowd if I hadn't left the damn thing at home.

Did my cell phone have a video function? I didn't know, which I should have. It just never occurred to me to figure it out since whenever I needed to videotape something, I knew I could use my camera.

Which was at home.

With my daughter, who was still waiting patiently on the phone.

"Hey, honey?" I said as I inched closer to the parking lot. The sirens were getting louder, and I saw the first flashing lights reflecting off the bank building's windows. "Can you do me a favor?"

"Um... sure?"

I hadn't seen Sewell in the crowd, but then again, he could be watching from inside the bank.

"Can you see if you can go over to Maddie's house for a while?"

She was quiet for a beat. "What's going on? All summer you've been weird whenever I want to go hang out with Maddie, and now you're..."

The first fire truck raced into the parking lot from the Virginia Street side, bouncing over a speed bump on its way to the burning car. Two police cars arrived on the scene. Ahead of me, the police began cordoning off the street.

"You want me out of the house," Samantha said.

I wasn't going to lie to her. "Just for a little while."

"Does this have something to do with Melody?"

"I'm not sure. It's just..." I didn't want to tell her that someone else associated with Melody had just been murdered in pretty much the same way. She'd be too worried about her dad. Hell, I was worried about her dad. "I'd feel better if you were at someone else's house until I make a few other calls."

I asked Samantha to call Maddie and then call me back to let me know if Maddie's mom could pick her up, then I disconnected. Traffic was so thick by now, I really needed to pay attention to my driving. Calling Norton would have to wait until I was through the worst of the traffic. I thought about going by his building, but there was no guarantee he'd be there. Better to connect by phone and arrange to meet later.

I gave up trying to scan the crowd for Sewell. There were too many people milling around, and too many cars on the street. I should have just headed on home, but I had to try.

Now that the initial shock had worn off, I was starting to get the shakes. A man I'd just spent time with was dead.

No, not just dead. Murdered.

At least this should get Ryan off the hook for Melody's murder. The way Melody and Richards had died was too similar to be a coincidence. Richards had spent years undercover in the drug scene, and now he'd been trying to dig up dirt on a money laundering operation involving an east coast mobster. He must have made some serious enemies along the way.

Besides, Ryan wouldn't have had any reason to murder Richards.

Except for the damn report I'd given him.

Crap.

I could just see how the cops would spin this. Overcome with grief and remorse after killing his fiancé following a very public fight, Ryan shifts the blame to the man he thought was stalking her. He tracks the man down and murders him in the same way he'd murdered his fiancé.

Would Ryan even know how to build a car bomb? I'd be willing to bet anybody could learn how to build a car bomb on the Internet.

That took care of motive and means, and as far as opportunity, I'd taken Richards on a car ride for almost an hour. Plenty of time for Ryan to plant a device in Richards' car.

Wait a minute.

*I'd* taken Richards on a car ride.

It hadn't been my idea—Richards had confronted me—but he was dead. I was the only one alive who knew I hadn't persuaded Richards to take a little ride with me.

I could feel the blood drain from my face. For the first time that day, the car's air conditioning felt too cold.

I could be in some serious trouble here, and not only from Justin Sewell. An undercover cop had been murdered. The security guard had seen the two of us together in the parking garage in what must have looked like the tense confrontation it had been. And the security guard wouldn't have any trouble identifying me if someone showed him my picture, not after my conversation with him yesterday.

I was already a person of interest in one murder. How big of a stretch would it be to connect me to this one?

Whether Richards had been well liked or not, he was still a cop. If Archulette or Squires thought they could pin an accessory charge on me, I might find myself on trial for something I didn't do.

I needed to talk to Kyle, and not just on speaker phone.

I drove down a few side streets, looking for a place where I could pull over and have a long conversation. The old houses in this part of town had been converted to office buildings, most of them home to small law firms. I'd done work for a lot of these firms. I wondered if any of them would still hire me if I was charged in connection with Richards' death, even if the charges were eventually dropped.

I was still looking for a place to park when a car slammed into me from behind.

## 27

I was so startled after the car hit me that for a moment I didn't know what to do.

I'd never been in a car accident before. I should knock on wood when I say that.

I know I've been incredibly lucky. I track down people who witnessed car accidents. I go to wrecking yards and take pictures of cars that are little more than lumps of twisted metal, and sometimes there's still blood on the metal. I live in a town where the streets are crowded with tourists who don't know where they're going, and with all that, I've never even been in a fender bender.

The car had hit me from directly behind for no apparent reason. I hadn't hit the brakes suddenly, and there was no other traffic on the street.

I'd stepped on the brakes out of reflex when the car hit me. I looked in my rearview mirror. The car behind me was a big old sedan, a Cadillac or Lincoln. An old guy in a straw hat was behind the wheel.

He must have seen me looking in the mirror because he held up both hands in an *I screwed up* gesture.

Okay, Abby. Think.

Turn on the flashers.

It took me a moment to find the right button on the dash, but I found it and switched on the warning lights.

Put the car in park.

That one was easy. I also put on the parking brake.

Take an inventory of yourself to make sure you're not hurt.

The collision hadn't been hard enough to really hurt me, but I turned my head and rolled my shoulders just to make sure. The shoulder I'd dislocated last December seemed a little tighter than normal, but it wasn't bad.

The next thing I needed to do was check my car and see if it was drivable. The car that had hit me was bigger than mine. I'd heard metal crunch. I was pretty sure it wasn't his bumper.

I looked in the rearview mirror to check for traffic before I opened my door.

The guy who'd hit me wasn't there.

Oh, great. A hit and run driver, and I hadn't even gotten his license plate number. Some investigator I was.

I slammed the car door a little harder than necessary as I got out to inspect the damage.

In the grand scheme of things, a hit and run fender bender wasn't worth getting upset about, especially when you've witnessed a murder and are pretty sure the cops are going to be arresting you, but sometimes it's the little things that can set you off.

Which, I supposed, was the reason I yelled at the old guy as he came trotting over to me from the little parking area beside one of the office buildings. He must have moved his car there so it wouldn't block the non-existent traffic on the street.

"Look what you did to my car!" I pointed at my poor car which now had definite dents in both the rear fender and the back of the trunk.

At least the panels covering the rear tires hadn't been

pushed in toward the tires, and I didn't see any liquid pooling out beneath the car. From my perspective, my car was still drivable.

"What in the world were you thinking?" I said. "And why did you move your car? We're going to have to report this."

I didn't wait for him to say anything. I walked around to the passenger side of my car where I'd left my purse and my cell. Here's hoping the cops hadn't already put out an arrest warrant for me. I was about to make it ridiculously easy for them to come pick me up.

I was so intent on getting my phone that I didn't realize the old guy had come up behind me until it was too late. I felt something solid press against the middle of my back. Something solid and metallic and cold.

"I was thinking this was a good way to introduce myself," he said.

I looked over my shoulder and realized with a shock that I'd seen this guy before, only then he hadn't been holding a gun. He'd been reading his tablet while he ate lunch at one of the outside tables at the cafe on California.

He was the old guy Justin Sewell had bothered as he'd stood in the doorway of the cafe taking pictures of Melody.

The same older guy Kyle had noticed in the photographs I'd taken. The guy Kyle said had looked familiar.

And I'd seen him since then. I'd passed him in the gym this morning when I'd talked to Stacy. I'd thought he'd looked familiar but I couldn't quite place him because he'd been wearing a baseball cap.

He'd made me, all right. He must have seen me drop Richards off while he was waiting for Richards to get back to his car. From there, it would have been pretty easy to follow me. Thank god I didn't go straight home.

He wasn't as old as I'd thought based on his picture. In person, his hair was more steel grey than white, and while his face was heavily lined, the lines were the kind caused by a life spent outside in the sun. His eyes were sharp, a cold ice blue, and his shoulders were a solid bulk beneath his loose cotton shirt.

The straw hat made him look older than he was, and the cotton chinos and canvas loafers made him look like a tourist. He could have doubled for any of a dozen senior citizens who get bussed into town on gambling junkets from California.

Only his accent gave him away. This guy was east coast through and through, and with the tan, I was guessing he made his home in Florida. Probably Boca Raton. Just like Gordino.

"We're gonna get in your car now," he said. "You're gonna climb over to the driver's side, and I'll be getting in behind you. Don't try anything foolish. I don't mind shooting a woman, but you probably figured that part out already."

I'd been kidnapped at gunpoint by a killer before. That time the guy holding the gun on me had been vicious and unpredictable. I'd only gotten out alive because I'd managed to pit him against his son, and even then I'd gotten very, very lucky.

The man holding a gun on me now wasn't vicious or unpredictable. He was doing a job. His job just happened to be killing people.

I didn't need an introduction to know that Gordino or one of his lieutenants had sent this guy out here to clean up after Sewell. He'd seen me with Richards, seen me taking pictures of Sewell, seen me talking to Stacy. As far as he was concerned, I was part of the mess he was supposed to clean up. It wasn't personal.

If I didn't do as he said, he'd shoot me in the back and walk away. If anyone saw anything, all they'd remember about the man who shot me would be that he was an old tourist in a straw hat. He probably had more than one change of clothes in his car. Put this guy in a suit and tie, and he'd look like a successful, middle-aged businessman. The last thing he looked like was a contract killer.

If I did what he said, he'd still kill me, but it wouldn't be immediately. Getting in the car would give me time to figure something out, and time was the only weapon I had.

I'd never tried to crawl over the center console in my car before. I'm not as young as I used to be. My legs didn't want to cooperate, but I finally managed to drag my feet the rest of the way over the shifter and right myself in the seat. The guy with the gun got in the passenger seat and shut the door after himself.

"Seatbelt," he said, gesturing at me with the gun.

I put my seatbelt on. He'd had me toss my purse and cell on the back seat. At least he hadn't destroyed my cell phone, but I couldn't reach it, just like I couldn't bail out of the car once I started driving. Not with the seatbelt holding me in place.

"The car's going to yell if you don't put yours on, too," I said. "Safety feature."

I expected him to give me grief, but instead he latched the seatbelt behind himself. He must have had practice since he managed to buckle the belt without putting the gun down. There are days when I have a hard time buckling the seatbelt even with both hands free.

So I was buckled in and he wasn't. This wasn't good. He'd prepared himself for a quick getaway. I wondered if he'd done the same thing when he had Melody drive to the place where he'd killed her.

He gestured at me with the gun. "Drive," he said.

I drove.

## 28

The railroad tracks that run through downtown Reno are no longer visible from street level, thanks to a handy-dandy covered train trench that cost the city way too much money and took far too many years to build. But even if you can't see the rails, Reno still has a right and wrong side of the tracks.

The contract killer sitting in the passenger seat of my car holding a gun trained on my midsection had told me to drive toward East Sixth Street, a place that was definitely the wrong side of the tracks.

Any number of abandoned properties on East Sixth would be a perfect place to kill me in my car without being spotted. He'd have plenty of time to plant an explosive beneath the seat and incinerate my car with what was left of me inside.

He hadn't carried anything into the car except the gun, but his cotton shirt was loose and he wore it untucked. He could be carrying what he needed in the pocket of his pants and the shirt would have concealed it.

"You killed Melody, didn't you," I said as I drove down Arlington toward Sixth.

"No talking," he said.

He was looking straight ahead, no doubt scanning the road to keep an eye on traffic while he kept one eye on me.

"Oh, come on," I said, sounding more confident than I felt. "You're going to kill me anyway. At least tell me the reason why. You owe me that much."

"You're a nosy broad. I don't like nosy broads. You want to stay on my good side, keep your mouth shut."

I opened my mouth to say something else, anything else, just to keep him talking, but he gestured at me with the gun.

I got the message. We were done talking. I wouldn't be able to distract him by getting him to tell me the whole story.

Not that I had a clue what I could do even if I did manage to distract him enough that he wouldn't shoot me the second I made a move. I couldn't punch him from where I sat, and even if I did manage to land a blow, it wouldn't have much force behind it. I'm not a fighter, and I don't have any martial arts skills. Maybe that was something I needed to learn if I got out of this mess alive.

My seatbelt was still snuggly buckled. I couldn't bolt from the car at a red light. Even if I could outrun a bullet, I'd have to be able to get out of the car first in order to try.

I doubted he would kill me in the middle of a busy city street, but I was pretty sure he could shoot me someplace that would hurt like hell but would let me keep driving, and no one would ever hear it. I might not know much about guns, but thanks to the movies, I could recognize a suppressor when I saw one.

I didn't have anything I could hit him with, either. No metal travel mug in the center console or heavy flashlight in the map pocket on the driver's side door.

I didn't even have a drink I could throw in his face. The iced tea I'd bought at the gas station was long gone. I had a couple of bottles of water on the floorboard on the back seat, but those would do about as much good as my cell phone.

He'd apparently been in town long enough to know his way around downtown. He told me to drive past Wingfield Park on Arlington. It was the most direct route to East Sixth, even though traffic slowed down around the park.

Wingfield Park had been built on a small island that bisected the Truckee River as it ran through downtown. The city had engineered this part of the river to provide a series of rapids for kayakers, and during the summer there were noon-time concerts in the park.

Today the park was full of locals and tourists alike seeking to beat the heat. I didn't come to the park nearly often enough. Whenever I was downtown, it was always for business.

If I got out of this mess in one piece, I promised myself I'd take more time to enjoy things like a walk in the park with my daughter or a Giants' baseball game with Kyle, even though I didn't like baseball.

We'd just passed the park when the chimes of the cathedral struck five o'clock. Saint Thomas Aquinas is an impressive two-story red brick building. I'd never been inside, but then again, I'd never been religious even though I'd been married in a church. Would it be sacrilegious to say a prayer now? I only had few more blocks to go before we hit Sixth.

Traffic had come to a stop as the cars ahead of me had to wait for pedestrians before they could make a right turn. I was more than content to wait—at this point every remaining minute of my life was pretty damn precious—but the guy who planned to kill me wasn't.

"Go around 'em," he said, gesturing with the gun. "Use the turn signal. No funny business."

No minor traffic infraction was going to save me, I guess.

I wasn't the only driver trying to get into the left-hand lane.

When I finally found a break in traffic and switched lanes, a driver coming up fast behind me leaned on his horn.

That attracted the attention of a police car I hadn't even seen going in the opposite direction. I saw the cop give me a long look as he passed me.

I held my breath and kept one eye on the rearview mirror. The steering wheel felt slippery beneath my sweaty palms. What would my unfriendly resident contract killer do if the cop turned around to follow me?

It turned out to be a moot question. The cop kept heading toward the river behind me, no doubt trying to catch speeders who failed to slow down for the fifteen mile-per-hour zone around the park.

"Don't try something like that again," my passenger said.

I could have protested my innocence, but what would have been the point?

We made it through the intersection and over the train trench behind the El Cortez Hotel. Traffic had thinned out a little, and my passenger had me switch back to the right-hand lane.

The half-full parking lot for the Sands was on my left and a motel about thirty years past its prime was on my right. The Sands always looked deserted to me compared to the bigger casinos only a block away. The best thing about the Sands were the chocolate milkshakes at Mel's Diner on the ground floor. I didn't want to think about the fact that I might never have another one.

Without warning, a car jetted out of the motel parking lot in front of me. I had to jam on the brakes to keep from hitting it.

Something rolled out from beneath my seat and hit the back of my left foot.

The can of pepper spray. It had to be. I'd forgotten that it had fallen beneath my seat when I'd been driving like crazy trying to catch a glimpse of the crowd around Richards' burning SUV.

Had my passenger seen it?

I risked a sidelong glance at him. He was busy staring ahead at the car I'd narrowly missed.

I shifted my left foot backwards just enough to push the can closer to my seat. I didn't think I'd be able to lean forward to reach it before my passenger shot me, but if I could get the can over to the side, I might be able to manage. Especially if he thought I was just adjusting my seat.

I dropped my left hand off the wheel and squirmed around in my seat.

He looked at me.

"The seat's off," I said. "It must have moved when you hit me."

"We don't have far to go," he said. "Leave it."

"If you don't want me to get in another accident, I need to have the seat in the right place. It'll only take me a second."

Traffic was slowing to a stop again in front of me. More cars waiting for pedestrians. So far he hadn't told me to go around like he had before. I slowed the car to a stop.

"Make it quick," he said. "Any don't try anything stupid."

I reached down beside my seat with my left hand and found the buttons that adjusted the position of the seat. I moved the seat forward. I hoped that I could shift the seat far enough forward to get my hand on the can of pepper spray without jamming the steering wheel into my chest.

Most of all I hoped I could make the whole thing look smooth enough he wouldn't know what I was doing.

It might have actually worked if I'd been wearing a long skirt. My jeans didn't conceal anything. He was watching me like a hawk, and he must have seen the metal can on the floorboard. Maybe he thought it was a gun.

"What the fuck did I tell you?" He aimed his gun at my legs.

"Let me see both hands right now or I blow your kneecap off. You only need one leg to drive."

He was right. My car was an automatic. I wondered what he would have threatened to shoot if I'd been driving a stick.

Even with a gun pointed at me, I had a sick feeling that this was the best chance I'd have to fight back. I'd actually managed to touch the can of pepper spray with my fingertips. Could I still grab it and spray him in the face even if he shot me? It would probably hurt worse than anything I'd ever experienced except maybe childbirth. I wasn't sure I could hold onto the can long enough to do anything if he shot me.

But if I didn't make a move now, what chance did I have when we got to wherever he was going to torch my car? He could shoot me as soon as I put the car in park and then take his time planting whatever device he had that would set my car on fire.

I was still trying to decide if I wanted to die with both legs intact when a police siren whooped to life directly behind me.

# 29

I'd been so intent on the killer in the passenger seat of my car that I hadn't realized a police car had pulled up behind me until the cop hit the siren and the lights simultaneously.

Even though the sudden noise scared the crap out of me, I was never so glad to see a police car in my life.

My passenger swore. "Don't do anything stupid," he said, gesturing with the gun.

Then he did something stupid instead. He glanced away from me to look at the police car in the side view mirror.

I didn't hesitate. I might die in the next few seconds, but I had to try.

I grabbed the pepper spray with my left hand and stomped on the gas.

The pickup truck in front of me was a king-cab diesel with a trailer hitch in the back. I said a mental apology to the driver as my car slammed into the back of the truck.

My car doesn't exactly go from zero to sixty in six seconds flat, but it had enough power that when I hit the truck, the force of the collision triggered both front airbags.

I'd been ready for the crash and my seatbelt kept me from kissing the steering wheel. When the airbag exploded out of the center of the steering wheel, it didn't punch me too hard.

My passenger wasn't as lucky.

He'd buckled his seatbelt behind himself for a quick getaway if he needed it. The collision threw him forward with nothing but the airbag to stop his forward momentum. When the airbag exploded out of the dash, it hit him square in the face.

Airbags can trigger with enough force to do serious damage when a person isn't wearing a seatbelt. If we'd been going freeway speed, the airbag might have killed him. As it was, I heard his shout of pain even over the grinding crash of metal on metal and the blare of my car's horn.

I hoped that the airbag at least broke his nose. Anything to give me even a tiny advantage over a guy who made a living killing people.

I knew that airbags were designed to deflate almost immediately. I'd told myself to be ready so I could aim the pepper spray at his face the minute the airbag was out of the way, but I was still only a split second quicker than he was.

That split second was enough. I managed to blast him square in the face with the spray before he finished raising his gun.

He yelled and clawed at his eyes with his free hand even while he fired his gun blindly.

The gun made little *pock, pock, pock* noises with each pull of the trigger. Most of the shots slammed into my dash or through the front windshield, but not all of the shots went wild.

A line of pain flared to life across the top of my thigh.

He was honing in on his target. If I didn't do something, the next shot would hit me in the ribs.

I flailed out with my right hand. I managed to hit the inside of his gun arm the same time he pulled the trigger, and the next shot tore through the top of the steering column.

I had to get out of the car. The space was too confined for the pepper spray. My own eyes were starting to burn. The windows were rolled up since I'd had the air conditioning on. The collision hadn't broken any of the windows. The only fresh air was coming in through the bullet holes in the windshield.

I dropped the can of pepper spray and used both hands to keep the guy's gun arm pointed away from me.

He was unbelievably strong, but I must have had all the adrenaline in the world coursing through me.

I yelled as I shoved as hard as I could, slamming his hand toward the dash.

The gun caught on the deflated airbag.

I let go of him and pushed the release on my seatbelt. I heard the catch give way.

I didn't check for traffic, didn't wait to see if he got control of the gun—I just opened my door and fell backward out of my car.

"Gun!" I yelled. "He's got a gun!"

I scrabbled backwards, trying to keep the bulk of my car between me and the gunman even though I'd seen his shots punch through metal.

A cop crouched down beside me, weapon drawn.

"He's got a gun," I said again.

"Is that your car, ma'am?"

The officer was a woman, sturdy and solid and serious.

"Yes," I said. My vision was starting to blur and my hands were shaking. "He hijacked me."

"Can you move?"

My thigh was wet with blood, but so far my leg still seemed to work. "I think so."

"Let's get you out of here."

With an arm around my shoulders, she hustled me behind

her patrol car, both of us crouched over as we ran as fast as my leg would allow. Once there, she called in the situation on the radio attached to her uniform.

I could hear more sirens closing in. She must have called for backup before I opened the door. Had she seen the gun? Or maybe she'd seen me pepper spray the guy.

"He's a pro," I told her. "I think he's got some kind of incendiary device. He was going to kill me and set fire to the car."

Her eyes narrowed. I could tell by the expression on her dark-skinned face that she'd made the connection. People didn't die in car fires every day in Reno. Whether or not she was directly involved in the investigation, I was willing to bet she knew about Melody's murder. I wondered if she knew Richards.

She crab-walked to the open door of her cruiser, and a moment later I heard her voice over a loudspeaker instructing everyone to clear the area.

I risked a peek around the driver's side of the cruiser. She was still crouched down, not giving the gunman a clear shot at her head. She was waiting for backup and protecting civilians. She wasn't going to play the hero and charge a professional killer with a gun.

I could understand that, but from her position she wouldn't be able to see if he did the same thing I'd done—simply bail out of the car and run away. Her cruiser was directly behind my car, and her view of the passenger side of my car was blocked.

I doubted getting caught and doing time was part of the gunman's plans. He couldn't afford to stay in the car, not with more police on the way.

If he got away, he'd be free to come after me again. Maybe next time he showed up in my life with a gun, Samantha would be with me. That thought was too horrible to contemplate.

I scooted around the back of the cruiser and peeked at the passenger side of my car just in time to see the door open.

"He's coming out!" I yelled.

A cloud of powder from the deployed airbags poured out the open door. It made the car look like it was already on fire.

The gunman rolled out much the same way I'd done, only he still had the gun. His straw hat was long gone and the lower half of his face was covered in blood leaking from his broken nose. He didn't look like a tourist now.

"Drop the gun," the officer said.

She wasn't using the loudspeaker anymore, but her voice was loud and clear and strong. I had no doubt that he'd heard her even over the blare of approaching sirens and the sounds of downtown traffic the next block over.

At least my car's horn was no longer adding to the din. Maybe he'd shot the horn to put it out of its misery, but I doubted he would have wasted the bullet.

He stayed crouched down, using my car as a shield much like I'd done. He was probably trying to decide if he should make a run for it.

Thankfully all the spectators who would normally hang around the edge of a collision had long gone, either because the cop had told them to leave or they'd heard me shout that he had a gun. There was no one within easy reach that he could use as a hostage or a human shield.

Then he looked my way, and I saw pure, raw fury steal the calm expression from his face.

I ducked behind the cruiser just in time.

A bullet slammed through the police car, exiting out the back of the trunk just a fraction of an inch away from my head.

He must have calculated where my head would be when I ducked away for cover, and he'd only been a hair's breadth off.

I flattened out on the ground as another bullet followed the first.

I couldn't run although every instinct in my body was telling me to run. I'd make a smaller target staying flat on the ground.

Provided he didn't scuttle down the side of the cruiser, out of sight of the cop, and just take me out as soon as he spotted me.

I twisted my head around and tried to peer beneath the cruiser. The hot asphalt burned my cheek, but at least I had a narrow view of the street beyond the cruiser.

The street, and a pair of canvas loafers.

He was doing exactly what I'd been afraid he would—crab-walking slowly toward the back of the cruiser.

"He's coming down the passenger side!" I yelled at the cop.

I rolled and tried to get my feet under me, but my abused thigh refused to cooperate. Instead of sprinting away, my leg almost collapsed beneath me.

I got ready to hit the ground and roll again when the cop's gun went off, a big booming sound compared to the return fire coming from the gunman.

I was in the middle of a shootout, and I was the only person without body armor or a gun. I'd never felt more helpless in my life.

The shooting stopped abruptly when the cavalry finally arrived on the scene.

Two more police cars skidded to a stop behind me. Car doors flung open and cops spilled out, pointing shotguns and handguns directly at me and the passenger side of the cruiser.

"Freeze!" one of the new arrivals yelled. He was a big Hispanic cop who probably bench pressed elephants in his spare time. His shotgun was pointed in my direction.

I would have liked to do nothing else except freeze only my body had other ideas.

I had just started to raise my hands up in the universal sign of *I give up, please don't kill me* when the world around me started to gray out.

Great. Just great.

I had just enough time to shift my weight so I wouldn't fall on my face—or my bad shoulder—before the gray turned to black, and I fainted right there in the middle of the street.

## 30

T he interview room in the F.B.I. field office didn't look that much different from the one in the downtown Reno Police Station. Plain walls, plain metal table, plain metal chairs. Norton sat beside me, but instead of Detectives Archulette and Squires, one lone F.B.I. agent sat across from us.

Special Agent McCarthy was a solidly-built forty-something. Dark hair, dark blue eyes, and the kind of chin that looked like it had been chiseled from granite. He could have been a model in a L.L. Bean catalog, except his stare would have given him away as something more than a handsome version of the guy next door who looked good in whatever he happened to be wearing.

Special Agent McCarthy was the kind of guy who could look at you and you'd swear he knew everything you'd done wrong your entire life. Evil Santa would have a stare like that.

"My client will be happy to cooperate," Norton said to McCarthy. "Provided we receive assurances that no charges—federal or local—will be pressed against her."

McCarthy didn't say anything. He just turned that stare on me.

My legs were trembling, and I couldn't put it all off to the ten stitches I had in the top of my thigh.

The doctor who'd stitched me up in the Emergency Room had told me I'd been lucky. He'd called it a "scratch." I was pretty sure scratches were the things I got from my cat, and so far I hadn't needed stitches for any of those.

The police had stood watch outside my cubicle in the Emergency Room. I'd been allowed to call Norton. After he'd arrived at the Emergency Room, I'd snuck in a call to Kyle, and then we'd all made a trek to the Federal Building where the Reno police handed me over—reluctantly, I thought—to Special Agent McCarthy.

I didn't think the police officers were entirely convinced that I'd had nothing to do with Richards' death. The cop who'd found herself in a shootout with the gunman who'd kidnapped me had originally pulled me over because a BOLO—be on the lookout—had been issued for me in connection with the explosion that killed Richards. I'd already been questioned in one car bombing, and the helpful security guard at the bank building where Sewell worked had recognized me when one of the cops who'd responded to the explosion showed him my picture, just like I knew he would.

Even I was impressed with how fast the cops had issued the BOLO for me. It had only been a minute or two old when the cop who'd pulled me over had spotted my car.

Any other day I would have freaked at the idea of being the subject of that kind of police attention. Today? Not so much.

By the time I'd recovered from my faint at the scene, I was in the back of an ambulance. I had an I.V. in my arm and a cold pack on my forehead.

The paramedic told me that between the blood I'd lost and the heat and the stress, he wasn't surprised I'd passed out.

They'd already treated two out-of-towners for heatstroke—one on a golf course and one fisherman trying to catch trout in the Truckee River west of town—and that I'd been lucky.

I supposed I had. The gunman could have killed me. I could have been killed in the crossfire.

The gunman hadn't been so lucky. I didn't know who shot him—the cop who'd pulled me over or one of the other cops who'd showed up right before I hit the asphalt—but he'd been pronounced dead at the scene.

I'd managed to have a quick conversation with Norton at the hospital before the police escorted me to my meeting with Special Agent McCarthy. I brought Norton up to speed, giving him the *Readers Digest* version of what Richards had told me about Melody and Sewell and the undercover operation the feds had going in their latest attempt to make some kind of charge against Gordino stick.

I also told him how the gunman had seen me taking pictures of Sewell and then seen me dropping Richards off, and that he'd probably jumped to the wrong conclusion—that I was part of the feds' undercover operation—and he'd decided to take care of me as well.

Norton wanted me to wait and see what the F.B.I.'s position was in all of this before I made an official statement. He doubted they'd be able to charge me with anything other than interference with a federal investigation, not that I'd done that intentionally, but he wanted to cut a deal just the same to make sure none of this could come back and bite me in the ass.

Norton also told me that the cops had issued a BOLO for Ryan in connection with Richards' murder. He'd briefly been in custody while I'd been at the hospital having my leg stitched up, but he'd been released when his alibi checked out. Ryan had been meeting with a funeral director planning Melody's services during the time that I'd taken Richards on a ride around the city. He couldn't have planted the bomb that killed Richards.

With Ryan off the hook for Richards, Reno P.D. had cancelled the BOLO on me as well. That didn't mean I was totally in the clear. There was still Melody's murder to consider.

Melody, who'd been Richards' snitch.

Who'd been Sewell's girlfriend, even while she'd been Ryan's fiancé.

"I can't speak for the local police," McCarthy finally said. He turned his gaze back to Norton. "I'm sure you realize that, Mr. Greenburger."

"Officially, yes. Unofficially?" Norton shrugged. "I've frequently been amazed at what a little inter-agency cooperation and goodwill can accomplish."

There'd been no inter-agency cooperation when it came to Kyle. He was currently cooling his heels in the waiting area.

If it had been Ryan, he would have been pacing. Kyle didn't pace. I knew he'd spend his time just sitting in one of the uncomfortable visitor chairs, his feet flat on the floor, back straight, seemingly calm and unconcerned.

I'd always thought I was pretty good at waiting, too, but my trembling legs said otherwise. I just wanted to get this over with and go home.

Provided my new home wasn't a jail cell.

"Give me a reason to make that happen," McCarthy said.

Norton leaned forward a little and gave McCarthy an icy stare of his own. "We all know what was going on here. Your operation was blown. The guys at the top were cleaning house. My client just happened to be in the wrong place at the wrong time. At the very most, all she's guilty of is being overzealous about doing her job. It's one of the reasons I keep offering her a permanent spot on my staff. Which, I might add, she continues to turn down, against all common sense."

To his credit, McCarthy didn't blink. "You know how this

goes, counsellor. I need something from you before I can go to bat for your client."

Norton had warned me that the feds would want a taste of the information I had to offer in exchange for immunity. I'd told Norton that I didn't have anything to use. All Richards had done was share the fact that his investigation existed. He didn't have any proof against Sewell when it came to money laundering—even Melody hadn't been able to get anything concrete against the man. Sure, he'd told me what Melody's assignment was supposed to have been, but that plan had died along with her. Richards couldn't prove that Sewell had anything to do with Melody's death.

What Norton wanted me to do wasn't exactly bluffing, but it was close. I'd warned him that I wasn't a good poker player, but I'd agreed it was the best piece of information we had.

"Melody went beyond what Richards told her to do," I said. "He wanted her to convince Sewell to buy her things, expensive things he'd need to dip into the boss's money to pay for. Enough money that it would be missed."

McCarthy just stared at me with those cold blue eyes. I wondered if he ever lightened up. Ever looked at something just for the enjoyment of it, not to try to dissect its truthfulness or usefulness.

I could tell he already knew that much. If Richards reported to McCarthy often, I wouldn't have anything at all to tell him. Norton and I were gambling that he hadn't told McCarthy everything that he'd told me.

"She decided she wanted to play a more active role," I said. "She went to that spy shop in midtown. Bought things that Richards didn't know about until after the fact. Decided to use them on her own."

The shift in McCarthy's expression was almost non-existent. His lower eyelids rose just a fraction, accompanied by a momentary pause in his steady breathing. If I hadn't been watching him closely, I would have missed it.

I'd scored a hit.

He sat without saying anything, clearly waiting to see if I'd keep talking to fill the silence. He didn't know me well. I used to be married to a lawyer. I knew how to keep my mouth shut, whether the silence was comfortable or not.

The silence stretched on long enough that I began to think of it like a staring contest. Who'd break first?

It wasn't going to be me.

I couldn't afford to let it be me.

McCarthy knew as well as we did that the spy shop sold all sorts of surveillance gear. As far as I knew, all Melody had done was make a copy of the key to Sewell's apartment. I kind of doubted that a woman who wanted to play spy would have stopped with a key, and I'd mentioned that to Norton.

That's when he'd decided that the key was the bit of information we'd keep to ourselves. He wanted to bait the feds with the information about the spy shop. He wanted them to assume, just like I had, that Melody had gone surveillance crazy on Sewell, only he wanted them to think that I knew all about it. We'd keep the little that I actually knew to ourselves until they came back with an immunity deal.

Of course, McCarthy or his minions could check with the spy shop to see what Melody had purchased, but that would take time.

Norton was gambling on the fact that the feds would be worried Sewell might disappear if he figured out he was the next guy on his boss's hit list. Norton had seemed confident that if the feds decided I had something worthwhile to deal with, something they could use to connect Sewell to Gordino, they'd want to make a deal quickly.

Me? I wasn't quite as confident, especially since it was my life on the line.

McCarthy eventually slid his chair back. If he was in a rush, he didn't show it.

"You'll have to excuse me for a moment," he said.

He got up with the casual grace of someone in superb physical shape. Almost everyone in my life was in better shape than I was. Even Norton.

I told myself that if I got out of this mess, I'd join a gym. Just not the one Melody had worked at. I doubted I could afford it.

After McCarthy left the room, Norton gave my hand a quick squeeze. He didn't smile or make any other gesture that would give me some idea how this was all going. He was probably a kick-ass poker player.

I couldn't ask him how he thought this was going either. The room didn't have any obvious surveillance equipment, but I had no doubt the F.B.I. could arrange to eavesdrop on conversations in its interrogation rooms without being blatant about it.

So I sat in my uncomfortable chair and waited. And waited.

The local anesthetic the emergency room doctor had used to numb my leg before he stitched it up had long since worn off. While my wound didn't hurt enough to make me want to climb the walls, I was more aware of it than I would have been if I'd actually had something else to keep my mind occupied.

"You called Samantha for me?" I asked Norton.

I'd been pushing it when I'd called Kyle in the hospital. I'd been out of touch with my daughter for hours now, and the last conversation I'd had with her hadn't exactly been reassuring.

"Kyle called her," Norton said. "Thought it would be better coming from him than me. Lawyers generally don't deliver good news." He raised his eyebrows apologetically. "Or at least that's been my impression when I call someone out of the blue." He squeezed my hand again. "She'll be fine."

She would be. She might have turned into a weight

conscious, fashion conscious teenager, but she was a strong kid. I just hated that she had to be so strong because of me.

But was it really all because of me?

It was easy to think, like Jonathan's mom apparently did, that I brought all sorts of trouble down on myself and my family because of what I did for a living. Except Ryan didn't do anything more dangerous than get in the middle of squabbles between business partners or insurance companies who couldn't figure out which one was really responsible for paying a claim. He certainly didn't do anything to deserve the grief he was going through. All he'd done was fall in love.

The news was full of gloom and doom and random acts of violence. It might seem like I had more than my share—two kidnappings in less than a year might make anyone wonder if she had her own personal little raincloud following her around —but safety, total safety, was an illusion.

The door to the interview room opened, derailing my thoughts. McCarthy took a step inside the room but didn't shut the door behind him.

"The Bureau would like to thank you for your cooperation," he said to me. "You're free to go."

## 31

I blinked. After all that strategizing, all that planning and worry and the police escort from the hospital to the F.B.I. field office, after all that waiting with my lawyer in an interview room, it all boiled down to Special Agency McCarthy thanking me for my cooperation and telling me I was free to go?

Beside me, Norton stood up. If his old bones were as stiff as mine, he didn't show it. "Thank you," he said to McCarthy.

Seriously. That was it?

I must have looked as confused as I felt. Norton held his hand out for me and gave me the slightest shake of his head.

I got the message: *Not here.*

I stood up, trying not to favor my wounded leg. "Thank you," I said.

McCarthy waited by the door for us to leave the room. He escorted us down the hall and into the waiting area.

I'd been wrong. Kyle must have been pacing. He was on his feet with his hands on his hips.

He didn't say anything, just gave me a hug and a quick kiss on the cheek, and we all left together.

The F.B.I. field office was in an innocuous-looking building in south Reno that looked like any other office building except for the bulletproof glass in the windows. By the time we got outside, it was nearly full dark, the sky a deep rosy lavender behind the mountains to the west. Most of the windows in the building were dark, the majority of the agents and support staff gone for the day, and those dark, bulletproof windows looked a little too much like malevolent staring eyes for my comfort.

That wasn't the best attitude for someone who occasionally worked with law enforcement officers—who was *dating* a police detective—to have, but I was just about fed up with the way the police and the Bureau had treated not only me, but Melody. I'm sure someone higher up the food chain would justify every-thing that had happened as being for the greater good, but they'd still used us in their attempt to hook a bigger fish.

As annoyed as I was about being used, I still didn't under-stand why they'd simply let me go.

Once we were out in the parking lot and away from the building, Kyle put an arm around my shoulders. "Anyone up for coffee?" he asked. "There's got to be a Starbucks around here somewhere."

I'd been given my purse and my cell phone at the hospital. That and my clothes were the sum total of the personal belong-ings I'd been allowed to take from the crime scene. My car had been impounded by the police. It was pretty much toast anyway, what with the damage from two collisions and all the bullet holes. My insurance company was going to have a field day with the claim.

I sighed. "Wherever we're going, I'm going to need a ride until I can arrange for a rental car."

Kyle grinned at me. "I think I've got you covered." He looked at Norton. "Coffee? I'm buying."

Kyle didn't usually drink coffee in the evenings. The fact that he'd mentioned it twice meant he wanted to have a conversation with the both of us, but he didn't want to have it in the parking lot.

Norton must have picked up on the subtext as well. "Best offer I've had all day," he said.

We found a Starbucks a few blocks away in a shopping center that also boasted a Walmart Supercenter and an abundance of fast food restaurants. I ordered an iced tea and lemonade combination while Norton settled for an iced decaf latte. Kyle was the only one who ordered coffee.

We sat at an outside table and watched the sporadic traffic go by. The valley was cooling off thanks to an evening breeze from the west. It made living in this desert town bearable during the summer, and sitting outside was pleasant even with the occasional blaring car stereo. Although after the day I'd had, anyplace where no one was holding me at gunpoint, shooting at me, or placing me under arrest was all right by me.

"So," I said, drawing the word out. "Don't take this the wrong way—I am definitely grateful to be here instead of back there—but what the hell just happened?"

Norton shared a look with Kyle. "They snagged a bigger fish," he said. "That's what I'm thinking. You?"

"Yeah," Kyle said. "That's my read."

"Gordino?" I asked.

"Not that big. I'm guessing Sewell turned himself in. He had a front row seat when Richards' car went up in flames with Richards inside. From what you've told me, Sewell is a smart guy. He can put two and two together, and he decided to cut himself a deal."

Norton nodded. "I agree. He might have had a contingency plan in place all along."

"But wouldn't he have done that after Melody was murdered?" I asked.

"Not necessarily," Kyle said. "Remember, RPD was looking hard at Ryan. Sewell had a sweet thing going. Criminals are a greedy bunch. He wouldn't have walked away from all that money unless he was sure Gordino knew he'd been skimming."

"But wouldn't he think Ryan might have killed Richards, too?" The police certainly had.

"Sewell could write Melody off as a crime of passion," Kyle said. "Richards was cold-blooded murder."

"That assumes Sewell knew Richards was using Melody," Norton said. "That Sewell knew Richards was undercover."

Kyle thought about that for a moment. Eventually he shook his head. "Not necessarily. Sewell was screwing Melody." He shot me a quick glance. "Sorry."

"No problem," I said automatically. I still had conflicted feelings about her, probably would have for a very long time, but none of that was Kyle's fault.

"Sewell had known Richards for a long time in connection with Richards' old RPD undercover drug cop gig. Sewell might have been playing Mr. Big Shot with both of them. Look," he said, and he started ticking points off with his fingers as he made them. "First, we know Richards was trying to get Melody to entice Sewell to overspend. Second, we know Richards had initially been trying to bust Sewell on drugs. Possession is a nice bust. Possession with intent is better. Interstate transportation gets you noticed by the feds. Third, we know Richards made himself a deal with the feds to go after Sewell. Who says it started with money laundering? Maybe the feds were interested in Sewell in connection with the drug trade, and along the way Richards stumbled on the possibility of an even bigger catch."

He glanced down at his fingers, frowning.

"Jeez, it might be later than I thought," he said. "I know I had a point here."

"You think Richards got Sewell to overspend on a drug buy," I said. "Or in connection with something to do with the drugs."

Kyle's frown disappeared. "Yeah. I do. If Sewell knew he'd

spent too much of the boss's money on his good friend Richards and his girlfriend Melody, the murder of both those people by the same method might have been enough to get his survival instincts to kick into high gear. Say what you will about the feds, their witness protection program is first rate."

"Witness protection," I said.

"It's the only way the feds can guarantee Sewell will still be alive to testify against his boss."

All that was well and good as far as speculating what happened with the F.B.I.'s interest in me—I doubted we'd ever know for sure—but that wasn't the end of my potential legal issues.

"What about the RPD?" I asked. "I'm pretty sure I'm not off the hook there."

Norton's expression turned serious. "They haven't officially charged you or Ryan, but you're right. The state's case is circumstantial at best. That doesn't mean they won't decide to pursue it."

"Ballistics," Kyle said.

We both looked at him. He shrugged.

"I pulled in a favor," he said. "Cops don't release all the details of a crime. We use it to double check supposed confessions or trip up suspects. The detail nobody released on Melody's murder was that she'd been shot."

I blinked. I knew cops withheld certain details, but that was a heck of a detail to hold back.

"They found a bullet?" Norton asked.

Kyle nodded. "She must have struggled. The bullet went through her and lodged in the engine block, but there's enough left that they'll be able to compare to the bullets recovered this afternoon."

I couldn't help but visualize what must have happened to Melody. Her car had been a brand-new Volkswagen Beetle. I didn't know much about Beetles except that the engine was in the rear of the car. The gunman had to have been practically on top of her when he fired.

Had she known she was about to die? I'd been terrified, but I'd known all along what the gunman planned to do to me.

At least he hadn't burned her alive like he had with Richards.

"What about the car bomb, for lack of a better word?" I asked. "Wouldn't he have used the same thing to torch her car that he planned on using on mine? Couldn't that be another way to prove that Ryan had nothing to do with Melody?"

Kyle shook his head. "I doubt it. The car fire was low tech. Book of matches, slow gas leak. I imagine the crime scene guys will find something a little more creative with Richards' SUV."

We all sat there for a while not saying anything.

A group of high school age girls came out of Starbucks, all holding large blended drinks, the kind that reminded me of coffee-flavored milkshakes. The girls were all thin and pretty and dressed in short-shorts and layered tank tops. They were chatting and laughing, and they didn't pay a bit of attention to us.

That was a good lesson to hang onto. My world had been turned upside down in the last couple of days. Ryan's had been shattered. And the rest of the world didn't care.

The case wasn't over yet, but based on what Kyle had told us, it would only be a matter of time. I'd done what I could to help Ryan. It nearly cost me my life, but in the end I was still here.

I squeezed Norton's hand. "Thank you," I said, the words far more heartfelt than the ones I'd said to Special Agent McCarthy. "I think I'm going to be working for you for free for the next year to pay off my legal bill, but thank you."

He gave me a tired smile and lifted his nearly empty latte. "Paid in full," he said with a nod at Kyle. "But if you tell any of my clients that I work for coffee, I'm going to double your bill."

I managed a weary laugh.

I had a daughter to pick up and a wounded leg to nurse, and I was going to need a new pair of jeans. The emergency room doctors hadn't shredded my pants to get at my leg, allowing me to take them off instead—something I was sure only happened when the wound was a "scratch"—but I was too old to start wearing jeans that had been distressed by bullet holes and blood stains.

At least, not on purpose.

"Well, okay then," I told Norton. "I hope you won't take this the wrong way, but I'm taking the rest of the week off."

## 32

The weather in San Francisco was clear and chilly with a stiff breeze coming off the bay. It was a good thing Kyle had warned me to bring a jacket and a sweatshirt. It had been in the high nineties in Reno the day before. It was in the low seventies in San Francisco, and where we stood at the far end of Pier 39 it was probably twenty below zero with the wind chill.

Kyle and I were doing the tourist thing. For the last hour we'd been wandering around Pier 39, doing more window shopping than actual shopping, although he had ducked inside a candy store to buy me an oversized lollipop.

The pier was crowded with Labor Day weekend shoppers. I'm not overly fond of crowds on my best days, and these weren't exactly my best days.

They were far from my worst either, a fact I had to remind myself of more than once when strangers bumped into me and I felt myself tense up.

At least my thigh had healed and the stitches were gone, although I'd always have a scar to remind me how close I'd come to losing my life.

Kyle had told me my feelings were normal given what I'd been through, and that the stress would eventually lessen and I'd start feeling like myself again. I wondered if he had first-hand experience with post-traumatic stress. We still had so much to learn about each other.

The crowd had thinned enough on the upper level of the pier that we'd been able to find a spot at the rail near an empty storefront that blocked the worst of the wind. Kyle was standing behind me, his arms wrapped around my waist, holding me close, as we watched the ships and sailboats on the bay.

This was the kind of thing I always used to do with Samantha, only I'd be the one standing behind her with my arms wrapped around her. Of course, that had been when she'd been younger and didn't mind being cuddled by her mother in public.

Samantha was currently spending a couple of days with Jonathan and his mother in Napa. This was supposed to be Ryan's weekend, but he wasn't up to having visitors yet. Melody's body had finally been released by the coroner only a few days ago, and her funeral would be next week.

Ryan and I had had several long talks. I'd listened to him while he raged at the cruel indifference of the universe and offered an understanding shoulder when he cried, and I never once told him what I'd learned about Melody and Justin Sewell.

Ryan had been through enough. He didn't need to know that the woman he'd loved hadn't been faithful to him. He especially didn't need to hear that from me.

Jonathan's mother and I had also spent some quality time on the telephone. She'd offered her condolences, and then she'd offered to host Samantha all of Labor Day weekend so that Kyle and I could still take our trip to San Francisco.

While I thought that was a generous offer, I didn't want to

impose. I also didn't want to leave Samantha in Napa all three days, at least not on her first overnight visit.

In the end, everyone had compromised.

Kyle had agreed we should cut our trip short, spending only one night in San Francisco. We'd dropped Samantha at Jonathan's house early this morning, and we'd be heading back to Napa to pick her up after tomorrow's Giants' game.

Samantha had wanted a longer visit, but considering she would be spending the better part of two days with Jonathan, she eventually realized she had a good thing going and didn't argue the point. Too much.

Besides, Jonathan's mother had told me he was saving up to buy a car. I had a feeling we'd be seeing a lot more of him as soon as he could drive himself to Sparks.

Of course, the inner voice of my mother was about as happy with the whole thing as Samantha was with the locked-down campus at her high school.

Whenever I doubted a parenting decision, that doubt took on my mother's critical voice. I didn't hear that inner voice as often as I used to—right after Ryan and I had separated my mother's voice had gone into hyperdrive—but apparently my first real bout of separation anxiety and empty nest syndrome was kicking in hard.

"Do you think she's having a good time?" I asked Kyle. "Samantha?"

He rested his chin in my shoulder. "She's spending two days with her boyfriend. Since you're spending two days with yours and you're still asking that question, should I be worried?"

I grinned and nudged his head with my own. "You know what I mean."

"I do."

I waited, but when he didn't say anything else, a niggling little worm of self-doubt started to burrow its way into my brain.

Kyle had left his own daughter behind. Lauren was spending the weekend with her mother. The two of them had shared custody of Lauren, which meant that Kyle spent a lot more time with his daughter than Ryan spent with Samantha. Maybe he was dealing with his own second thoughts about spending the weekend so far away from her.

"How about you?" I asked. "Should I be worried whether you're having a good time?"

He hugged me closer. "I am endeavoring to enjoy the moment," he said.

Endeavoring?

I pulled away a little so I could turn my head and look in his eyes.

Kyle had the most gorgeous eyes of any man I'd ever met, including Ryan. I'd seen him shut down emotionally when he was in cop mode, his eyes as flat and blank as his expression, and I'd been lucky enough to have him look at me with the kind of soul-baring gaze that took my breath away. Now his eyes looked troubled.

"What's up?" I asked. If it was something bad, I didn't really want to know, but I didn't want to put it off either.

He hesitated for a moment, and I felt my heart grow as cold as the wind off the bay.

Kyle was the first person I'd dated since my divorce. While I had no reason to think that it would turn into anything special or long-lasting, I didn't want our relationship to crash and burn either.

"I never really understood how Ruth felt," he said slowly. "Every time I'd go out on a call."

Ruth was his ex-wife. He'd still been a patrol officer when they'd divorced.

"She worried about you," I said.

"Drove her nuts. I was pretty cavalier about it, I guess. Hot shot young cop. Didn't really think about what it must have been like for her."

He'd told me before that his ex couldn't handle the stress of being a cop's wife, and it had driven them apart. From what I'd seen so far, they seemed to have an amicable enough divorce as divorces go.

Kyle glanced at the bay, like he didn't want to look at me. "Got a taste of my own medicine, as my dad would have said."

He'd asked me to back off my investigation and I hadn't. I couldn't have backed off, not if I wanted to live with myself. I hoped now that my decision hadn't driven a wedge between us.

This was the same kind of conversation I'd had with Jonathan's mother. I just never expected to have it with Kyle.

He put his life on the line all the time. Maybe not as much as patrol officers who never knew what kind of trouble they were walking into whenever they got a call about a domestic disturbance or a man with a gun. But Reno had its own share of random violence these days. Cops and private investigators weren't the only ones who risked their lives every time they stepped outside.

"You can't keep me safe," I said. "Nobody can. I could get hit by a drunk driver tomorrow, or go to the bank on the wrong day and get killed during a robbery. Even if all I do for the rest of my life is chase after guys who file phony insurance claims, there's no guarantee I won't rub a con man the wrong way someday and make him think he can take his frustrations out on me."

He gave me a smile that was more than a little on the rueful side. "Seems I've heard something along those lines."

I didn't doubt it. I grinned back. "Oh you have, have you?"

"Yes." He kissed me on the lips, a light, tender kiss. "So, I am endeavoring to enjoy this moment with you, and the next, and the one after that, and forget that you have a job that can be as dangerous as mine."

So far I hadn't found myself worrying about the dangerous aspects of his job. Was it different because we weren't living together? Hadn't really committed to each other as a couple? Would that change when we did?

I stopped myself. Wasn't I just thinking not five minutes ago that I didn't have any reason to think that our relationship would last? Now here I'd gone and thought *when*, not *if*.

I had to admit it was a pretty darn pleasant thought.

"What?" he asked.

I made an inquisitive sound.

"The look on your face," he said. "Made me wonder what you were thinking about."

I might have been a newbie at this dating thing, but I knew enough not to mention I was contemplating couplehood. At least, not yet.

"I was thinking about those moments," I said. "Especially the ones we're going to have tonight."

It was only a small fib, and besides, I had been thinking about the moments we'd have tonight ever since we'd decided to take this trip. Tonight's moments, and tomorrow morning's moments when we'd be waking up together for the first time.

"Oh," he said, his grin melting into something more intimate. "Nice way to change the subject."

He kissed me again, a little more seriously this time. A preview of those moments to come? I sure hoped so.

When we stopped, he glanced down at the oversized lollipop I was holding. "So, I plied you with candy, I've promised to buy you genuine San Francisco sourdough and a shrimp cocktail, and we can even ride the cable car back to the hotel if you want."

He had done all those things. I arched an eyebrow, wondering where this was going.

"Think you might reconsider wearing a Giants' hat tomorrow?" he asked.

He looked so hopeful, I had to chuckle. Yes, I looked horrible in a baseball hat, but for him? Relationships were all about compromise, and as compromises went, this was a little one.

"If you take my picture," I said, "you might have to arrest me for assaulting an officer."

"Was that a yes?"

I held up the lollipop. "This had better be one fantastic lollipop."

"I have it on the highest authority that it's the best lollipop in San Francisco," he said.

"The highest authority?"

He shrugged. "The girl behind the counter."

"An unimpeachable source."

"Of course."

He was grinning down at me, and I saw it again—that open, honest expression in his eyes that made my heart do strange things.

Maybe it was the city, or the fact that we could just be two people here, not the detective and the private investigator we had to be back home, or that I'd come so close to losing my life, but I couldn't remember the last time I'd felt so alive. Alive and happy and cared for.

When my mother's voice tried to pop up in my head and ruin the moment, I squelched that bit of negativity and worry.

This might be only the start of a deeper, long-lasting relationship with Kyle, or it might be the best day I'd have with him. Either way, for right now, life was good.

And you know what?

I intended to enjoy the heck out of it for however long it lasted.

# NEWSLETTER SIGN UP

Be the first to know!

If you love Annie's writing, her newsletter is a great way to keep up with new releases, special promotions, and bundles where her work is featured. Not to mention the occasional giveaway that's only available to her newsletter subscribers!

You'll even receive a free copy of the first Abby Maxon mystery novel, *Pretty Little Horses!*

What are you waiting for?

Sign up at https://anniereed.wordpress.com/newsletter/ today!

# ABOUT THE AUTHOR

A prolific, versatile, and award-winning writer, Annie Reed's written more short fiction than she can count. She's a frequent contributor to *Fiction River, Pulphouse Fiction Magazine*, and *Mystery, Crime and Mayhem*. She's a multiple Derringer awards finalist, and her short mystery fiction has appeared in year's best volumes, including both Year's Best Mysteries for 2023. She's even had her work selected for inclusion in study materials for Japanese college entrance exams. Her *Unexpected* series of short-story collections showcase some of the best of her work.

Annie's a founding member and contributor to the to the innovative Uncollected Anthology series of themed urban and contemporary fantasy anthologies. She writes mystery, science fiction, and fantasy novels under her own name and suspense novels as Kris Sparks. She also writes the Liberty Springs sweet romances under the name Liz McKnight. She can be found on the web at https://anniereed.wordpress.com/.

*A Special Request from the author:*

Word of mouth is critical for any author to succeed. If you enjoyed this book, please consider leaving a review at the site where you purchased it. Even a line or two would make all the difference in the world and I would greatly appreciate it.

Thank you!